Dawn and the We ♥ Kids Club

**Other books by
Ann M. Martin**

Rachel Parker, Kindergarten Show-off

Eleven Kids, One Summer

Ma and Pa Dracula

Yours Turly, Shirley

Ten Kids, No Pets

Slam Book

Just a Summer Romance

Missing Since Monday

With You and Without You

Me and Katie (the Pest)

Stage Fright

Inside Out

Bummer Summer

BABY-SITTERS LITTLE SISTER series
THE BABY-SITTERS CLUB mysteries
THE BABY-SITTERS CLUB series
(see back of book for a more complete listing)

Dawn and the We ♥ Kids Club
Ann M. Martin

AN
APPLE
PAPERBACK

SCHOLASTIC INC.
New York Toronto London Auckland Sydney

Cover art by Hodges Soileau

ISBN 0-590-47010-8

12 11 10 9 8 7 6 5 4 3 2 1   4 5 6 7 8/9

Printed in the U.S.A.   40

First Scholastic printing, February 1994

The author gratefully acknowledges
Peter Lerangis
for his help in
preparing this manuscript.

Dawn and the We ♥ Kids Club

CHAPTER 1

"Okay, guys, you're history," said my math teacher, looking at the wall clock. "See you *mañana*."

It was the end of a long school day. I chatted with friends as I left class, then got some books from my locker. As I walked outside, the midwinter breeze felt warm and wonderful.

Time out. What's wrong with this picture?

Number One: no obnoxious bell at the end of school.

Number Two: no coat.

Number Three: no cold weather.

Welcome to California!

I, Dawn Schafer, was back in my home state — the land of beaches and surfing and palm trees and year-round tans. Well, that's an exaggeration. It's a stereotyped idea of California. Nevertheless, it was a different life.

Different from Stoneybrook, Connecticut, that is. That's where I live, technically. This trip to California is sort of an extended visit.

Confusing? Not really. I am a child of divorce. My mom lives in Stoneybrook and my dad lives here in Palo City, California. (Once upon a time we all lived in Palo City. I was born here and so was my younger brother, Jeff.)

The divorce happened when I was in the seventh grade. Mom whisked Jeff and me off to *her* hometown, Stoneybrook, mainly because her parents — my Granny and Pop-Pop — still live there.

I liked Stoneybrook right from the start. We moved into a rambling old farmhouse built in 1795, where I found a secret passageway from the barn to my bedroom! I made some great friends at my new school, and I joined a group called the Baby-sitters Club (I'll tell you about them later).

As for Jeff, well, he was miserable. He was rude and difficult at home, and he even started getting into trouble at school. Eventually Mom and Dad agreed he'd be better off back in California. Boy, was it hard to see him go. Our house seemed so empty.

But not for long. Mom got married again — to the widowed father of my best friend, Mary Anne Spier. It turned out Mom used to date him in high school. (Isn't that *so* romantic?) Mary Anne and her dad moved into our house, and suddenly I had a nice, cozy, new family. My life couldn't have been better.

Except when I started thinking about Dad and Jeff.

And thinking. And thinking.

And missing them more and more.

Imagine if *your* dad and *your* only brother lived three thousand miles away. Let me tell you, it feels awful. I'd visited them a couple of times, but that just wasn't enough. I felt as if they were in another world, floating away from me. I needed to spend some time out West. A lot of time.

Mary Anne cried when I told her how I was feeling, but she understood. Poor Mom — she took it personally at first. When she phoned Dad about it, they argued. But that didn't stop them from exploring my idea. They had to consult guidance counselors at Stoneybrook Middle School *and* at Vista, my California school, to make sure I wouldn't screw up my education if I moved. Then, finally, they agreed I could live with Dad for six months or so.

Which is how I became bicoastal. (I love that word. It sounds so glamorous.)

To be honest, it isn't very glamorous at all, but you know what? Coming out here was definitely the right thing to do. That aching feeling is gone. It's fun to be around Dad, and

I no longer miss Jeff (honestly, I want to throttle him sometimes).

"Hey, Dawn!" a voice called from behind me.

I turned. Our school is actually a bunch of small buildings grouped around a courtyard filled with flowering bushes and juniper trees. Walking across the courtyard were two of my best California friends, Sunny Winslow and Maggie Blume. Sunny was holding out an open bag of vegetable chips.

"Hi!" I called back.

"Want some?" Sunny asked.

"Sure!" Yum. Vegetable chips are the best. They're like potato chips, except they're made with carrots and parsnips and sweet potatoes and other great stuff.

Okay, stop gagging. I just happen to like natural foods. That's one thing you should know about me. Luckily, most of my friends here share my tastes, too. (Most of my Stoneybrook friends don't. Mary Anne's boyfriend says I go around gathering nuts with the squirrels, but that's typical boy humor, and I ignore it.)

Having best friends on both coasts is pretty fantastic. Not to mention belonging to two great baby-sitting clubs.

That's right. I am a bicoastal baby-sitter. Here in Palo City, I belong to the We ♥ Kids

Club (pronounced "We Love Kids Club"). Sunny started the club while I was living in Stoneybrook, after I'd told her about the BSC.

Maggie's a member of the club, too, along with one other girl, Jill Henderson. (Jill lives pretty far from school, so she takes a bus home.) All four of us have blonde hair. Actually, my hair is the lightest (it's almost white). I suppose we could call ourselves the BSC, too, for "Blonde Sitters Club."

Or maybe OFEC, for "Organic Food Eaters Club." Sunny, Maggie, and I tore into those chips on our stroll down Palm Boulevard. It was one of those breezy, warm days when you just feel like doing nothing, and slowly. The sun beamed down and the air was full of familiar southern California scents: flowers, salt air, and car exhaust. (Oh, well, I guess no place is perfect.)

"You guys want to have a meeting today?" Sunny asked.

Maggie nodded. "We haven't had one in a week."

"I can't make it," I said. "I have to sit for Stephie. How about tomorrow?"

"Sounds cool to me," Maggie replied.

"I'll call Jill," Sunny offered.

Pretty casual, huh? That's the We ♥ Kids Club — no rules, no regularly scheduled meetings. *Much* different from the BSC. If Kristy

Thomas, the BSC founder, had heard that conversation, she would have had a heart attack. She's a real rules freak. The Baby-sitters Club is run like a business, with strict meeting times, officers, and record-keeping.

I have to admit, at first I had trouble getting used to the easy-going W♥KC style. Now I find it kind of refreshing.

Anyway, we yacked and munched for about ten more minutes, until we reached Stephie Robertson's house. I said good-bye to my friends and rang the bell.

"Dawn! Dawn! Dawn! Dawn! Dawn! Dawn!" Stephie screamed from inside.

Stephie is an only child and her dad is a widower. Her regular nanny, Joanna, usually sits for her. But tonight Joanna was leaving early, to celebrate her birthday.

The screen door opened and out Stephie flew. "Come *on!*" she said, pulling me inside. "You have to see Joanna. She looks so beautiful!"

Joanna came in, dressed in a short fringed skirt and a tight-fitting beaded top, her dark hair pulled back in a sleek, elegant style. She did look great, but also a little embarrassed, as we oohed and aahed over her. Joanna and I quickly went over some last-minute details. Before long, a car pulled up to the curb, with a very handsome man behind the wheel.

As Joanna climbed in and waved good-bye, Stephie said, "That's her boyfriend. He's a hunk."

I couldn't help laughing. "Stephie, where did you learn that word?"

"*Dawwwn,*" she said, rolling her eyes, "I *am* eight years old."

"Oh."

"It *does* mean something good, doesn't it?"

"Uh, well, sure . . . I guess."

"Like what?"

I have to say, Stephie is another reason I like being in California. She is the sweetest, smartest girl I have ever sat for. She used to be painfully shy, but as you can see, she's starting to come out of her shell.

Since she was little, Stephie has suffered from asthma. Emotional stress can send her into a scary fit of wheezing. Fortunately that seems to be getting better, too.

Halfway through my explanation of "hunk," Stephie lost interest. "Let's bake," she said. "Dad and I got a cake mix for Joanna's birthday. To surprise her when she gets back later. I want it to be huge. Like, *nine* layers!"

Fortunately the box had enough mix for *two* layers (which was plenty). So we spent the rest of the afternoon in the kitchen. Stephie had the best time. Me? I was grossed out. Do you know how much refined sugar goes into a cake? Tons! I mean, humans were not *made* to consume that much.

Sigh. Try telling that to an eight-year-old. Stephie thought I was out of my mind.

When we were done, the house smelled . . . well, *sweet*.

I hope Stephie was able to keep her dad away from the cake. You should have seen his face when he came home. He was practically drooling.

As for me, I couldn't wait to get to my house and make a fruit smoothie in the blender.

My dad's house is about a fifteen-minute walk from Stephie's. It's beautiful — airy, open, and shaped like a square-edged U around a yard. Almost all the rooms have glass skylights. I love coming home to it.

I ran up the front walk and through the door. "Hi! I'm home!" I called out.

"No you're not. You're *Dawn!*"

That was my brother, Jeff. He had decided the week before that he wanted to be a stand-up comedian. I'd heard that joke five times already. I vowed to myself I would never say "I'm home" again.

"Hi, Jeff," I replied, not encouraging him.

But he barged into the living room, determined to continue the act. "Dawn, what do you call a Smurf in math class?"

I walked around him toward the kitchen. "I give up."

"*A Smurf bored!*" he said triumphantly, cracking up. "Get it? Like a *surfboard!*"

Our housekeeper, Mrs. Bruen, was preparing a salad in the kitchen. "Hello, sweetheart," she said softly. "Just be glad he's not doing those knock-knock jokes — "

Too late. "Knock-knock!" Jeff said.

"Who's there?" I asked wearily.

"Kook."

"Kook who?"

Jeff looked at his watch. "Only one o'clock? Hmm, my watch must be wrong. . . . *Get it?* You said *cuckoo*, like a cuckoo clock!"

(Ugh. Brothers. Sometimes I wonder why I ever left Stoneybrook.)

This went on for a while, until Dad got home from work. "Hello, everybody!" he called as he came inside. *"I'm home!"*

He did it on purpose. I know he did. He *wanted* Jeff to give his dumb response.

"No, you're not — "

I put my fingers in my ears.

Dad is one of the nicest guys in the world. Too nice sometimes. He thinks Jeff's new joke habit is just terrific. He laughs at the same lines over and over. (But I love him anyway.)

"How's my Sunshine?" he asked, giving me a kiss. "Ready for my award-winning vegetable *chimichangas* tonight?"

Without waiting for an answer, he bounded away to change clothes. I guess I would have said yes to the question. Dad *is* a great cook. But I do have mixed feelings about his *chimichangas*. You see, they happen to be the favorite dish of his girlfriend, Carol. When he makes them, it's a sure sign she's coming over.

Have I mentioned Carol? Maybe not, but I guess I should.

Now, don't get me wrong. I like her. She has many good qualities. She's young and tries to be hip, she has tons of energy, and she pays lots of attention to Jeff and me.

Her bad qualities? Well, she's young and tries to be hip, she has tons of energy, and she pays lots of attention to Jeff and me.

What I mean is, she tends to go overboard. Sometimes she tries so hard to be cool it drives me crazy. I just want to tell her to act like a grown-up.

When Dad returned to the kitchen, we all set to work. Mrs. Bruen chopped veggies, Dad seasoned the sauce and made refried beans, I fixed a salad dressing, and Jeff cooked the rice.

Sure enough, at six o'clock on the dot, Carol's voice called from the front door,

"*Chimi*chang*as!* Mmmm, that smells *soooo* bodacious!"

Bodacious? Now you see what I mean.

"Hi, honey!" Dad said. "We need your expert taste buds."

Carol bustled into the kitchen. "Oh, you know I have good taste. I met you, right?"

She giggled. Dad laughed. They kissed.

Me? I managed to hold on to my appetite. But it wasn't easy.

Between Jeff's jokes, Dad's encouragement of him, and Carol's constant giggling, I didn't say too much at dinner. Which was just as well. The meal was fantastic.

But afterward I felt a little down. I guess I'd been hoping for a nice, quiet dinner.

I knew one thing that would cheer me up. "Dad, can I call Mary Anne?" I asked.

"If it's not too late," he said.

I looked at the clock: 7:03. That meant 10:03 at night in Connecticut. I raced into Dad's bedroom and tapped out my Stoneybrook number.

"Hello?"

I was in luck. Mary Anne was up. "Hi!" I said. "It's Dawn! Are you sleeping?"

"No, I'm reading," Mary Anne replied. "How are you?"

"Fine. What are you reading?"

Mary Anne laughed. "Is that why you called?"

"No. I guess I just wanted to, you know, *talk*."

"Okay. Well, it's the coolest book. It's called *Julie of the Wolves*."

Mary Anne went on about this book, which is the story of a girl lost in the wilderness of Alaska. I'd read it already, but I listened anyway. It was so great to hear her voice. She is the kindest, most sensitive, and most wonderful person in the world.

I don't know exactly why, but I was missing her — and my Stoneybrook family — more than ever that day. And the phone call was only making it worse.

CHAPTER 2

"**B**end your *knees*, Jill. Like this." Sunny got on her surfboard and demonstrated proper body balance.

No, we weren't at the beach. We weren't even outdoors. Sunny was giving a surfing lesson on the carpet of her own bedroom.

The We ♥ Kids Club had finally gotten around to holding a meeting. It was Tuesday, five days after I'd sat for Stephie. I had arrived right on time, at 4:30. Jill was next at 4:36, Maggie at 4:40.

No one complained. (If this happened at a BSC meeting, Kristy would be furious.)

"Go ahead, try again," Sunny insisted.

"This is ridiculous," Jill mumbled. She stepped on the board, which began to wobble left and right. So she flapped her arms wildly and gave us her version of the theme song from *Hawaii Five-O.*

We howled. "Perfect!" Sunny exclaimed.

Sunny is my oldest friend in the whole world. Well, she's not *old*. She's thirteen and in eighth grade, like me. What I mean is, I've known her the longest. We have lots in common. First of all, we're both outgoing, fun-loving, and independent. Second, we both have blonde hair, although Sunny's hair is strawberry-blonde and mine is almost white. Third, we share the same name, sort of (by pure coincidence, "Sunshine" happens to be my dad's nickname for me). Fourth, we like to surf. And fifth, we adore ghost stories.

The Winslows live down the block from us. Their house is like my second (I mean, *third*) home. You should meet Mrs. Winslow. She's a potter who makes the most beautiful stoneware — plus she's one of the warmest people I've ever met.

Sunny's full name is Sunshine Daydream Winslow. Yes, I am serious. (Mr. and Mrs. Winslow were hippies. Their friends in Oregon, the Johnstons, have two sons named Vernal Equinox and Lunar Eclipse.)

Hey, don't ask *me*.

Jill Henderson is actually quiet and serious when she's not carpet-surfing. Of all of us blondes, she has the darkest hair, and deep, chocolatey brown eyes. She's the only one who doesn't live in the neighborhood. Her house is tucked away in the hills at the edge of town. Her parents are divorced, so she lives with her mom and her older sister, Liz. They have three dogs — all boxers — named Spike, Shakespeare, and Smee. (Jill loves them, but boy, are those dogs ugly.)

I guess Maggie has the most glitzy life of us all. Her dad is in the movie business. I'm not exactly sure what he does, but it must be important. You would not believe their house. It's enormous, with a screening room, a gym, and a landscaped pool that looks as if someone lifted it from a tropical island and plopped it in their backyard. But you know what? Maggie hates talking about celebrities and movie gossip. Keanu Reeves has actually had dinner at her house, but she didn't tell us until weeks later. To her, it just wasn't a big deal. (Sunny, on the other hand, insisted on touching the fork and plate he used.)

Maggie has the coolest look (which is constantly changing). Her hair is short and punkish, with a thin tail in back. She usually streaks it purple or green or black. Her fashion sense runs toward leather bomber jackets and lace-up black boots.

What happens at a W♥KC meeting (besides surfing)? Well, we talk, snack, and answer some phone calls for baby-sitting. Neighborhood parents can count on us whenever they need an experienced and reliable sitter.

Great idea, huh? Little do any of the local parents realize that they have Kristy Thomas to thank.

That's right. As far as I know, no one had ever dreamed up a baby-sitters club before Kristy did. She's amazing that way. Ideas burst out of her all the time.

She invented the BSC to help her mom, who was a single parent trying to raise four kids. Since then Mrs. Thomas has gotten remarried, to a really rich guy named Watson Brewer, who had two kids from a previous marriage. Now the family lives in a mansion — with an adopted little sister, a grandmother, and several pets.

Kristy has brown hair and brown eyes, is great at sports, and always dresses casually. Although she's the shortest BSC member, she has the strongest personality. In case you haven't guessed, she's the club president.

Every BSC member has a title and certain duties. The club meets from 5:30 to 6:00 on Mondays, Wednesdays, and Fridays. Parents know to call only during those times. The club advertises around town and has *tons* of clients. How do they keep track of all of them? With another Kristy invention: the club record book, which has a client list and a calendar of our

16

appointments. Club members also have to write about each sitting experience in the club *notebook*. (Yup, Kristy's idea, too.)

If the BSC were a car, Kristy would be the starter — but Mary Anne would be the engine. As club secretary, she keeps things running (she's in charge of the record book). Kristy and Mary Anne are best friends. They even look alike, although Mary Anne's brown hair is cut really short these days. Personality-wise, they couldn't be more different. Mary Anne is quiet and super-sensitive. It doesn't take much to make her cry. Her boyfriend, Logan Bruno (the one who calls me "Runs With Squirrels") carries a box of tissues when they go to movies together. Needless to say, she is the world's best, most caring sister. Before our parents married, she never had a sibling or a mother. Her mom died when she was a baby, and Mr. Spier raised her by himself — *very* strictly, too. (Fortunately, being married to my mom has loosened him up.)

Claudia Kishi is the club vice-president, mainly because her room is BSC headquarters. She's Japanese-American and absolutely *stunning* (thin, too, despite the fact that she's a junk-food fanatic). Claudia is the most talented person I know — in drawing, painting, sculpting, jewelry-making, even fashion. She can create the coolest outfits out of odd combinations of clothes. Her spelling is creative, too — and her math. In other words, Claud is not a great student. Her parents used to wish she could be more like her older sister, who's a real genius, but I think they've given up comparing.

The BSC's other fashion-plate (and treasurer) is Stacey McGill. She's very sophisticated, but not snobby. She was born and raised in New York City, and her dad still lives there (she's another "divorced kid"). Her duty is collecting dues on Mondays and paying our expenses — like Claudia's phone bill. Stacey and I have some important things in common: divorced parents, blonde hair (hers is darker), and healthy eating habits. She has no choice about *her* diet, though, because she's diabetic. That means her body can't control the amount of sugar in her blood. She can't eat sweets, and she injects herself daily with a substance called insulin. (I know, it's gross, but she can't help it.)

Oh. My BSC title was alternate officer. I could take over anyone else's job in case of emergency.

All the BSC members are eighth-graders, except for Jessi Ramsey and Mallory Pike. They're our junior members, and they're both in sixth grade. They usually take early sitting jobs, since they have strict curfews. (Hating their curfews is one of the many things they have in common.) Talk about talent — Jessi's a gifted ballerina, and Mallory writes and illustrates her own stories. Jessi is the club's only African-American, and she had to deal with a lot of prejudice in Stoneybrook when her family moved in. She's the oldest of three kids. Mallory is the oldest of *eight* kids, so she's kind of a round-the-clock baby-sitter. Lately, Mal's been recovering from mono, so she hasn't been active in the club.

How does the BSC deal with two absent members (Mal and me)? By relying on its two *associate* members. Normally the associates take occasional jobs and are excused from attending meetings. But nowadays one of them, Shannon Kilbourne, has taken over my job as alternate officer. Shannon's the only BSC member who goes to a private school (Stoneybrook Day School). She's involved in all kinds of extracurricular activities there. I don't know how she finds time for everything.

The other associate is Logan Bruno. Yes, Mary Anne's boyfriend. Even though he's a carnivore and a jock, I like him. He talks in this cute Kentucky accent, and he's great-looking. He's been handling some of the sitting overload, too.

I've been in touch with all the BSC members, but mostly with Mary Anne. They're all, like, flabbergasted that the We ♥ Kids Club has lasted without strict rules.

It is pretty amazing when you think about it. Parents can call any of our numbers whenever they want. Whoever gets the call takes the job, or lines up someone else. Sunny has a record book at her house but we don't use it much, since the calls come in at all our houses. Somehow we always seem to work things out.

Our meetings, as you've already seen, are very casual. (Sometimes we even hold them outside.) Officers? No way. Punctuality? It might as well be a foreign word.

Bleeeep! The phone chirped as Sunny was explaining to Jill about waxing surfboards.

Sunny grabbed the receiver from her night table. "We Love Kids Club," she said. "Hi, Mr. Robertson. . . . Yes, we're all here. . . . A week from Saturday? Hang on."

(At this point in a BSC meeting, Claudia would tell the parent she'd call right back. Then she'd hang up while Mary Anne was carefully looking through the record book, checking every possible scheduling conflict and trying to make sure each member was getting a roughly equal amount of work.)

Not the We ♥ Kids Club. "Dawn, are you busy that day?" Sunny asked with her hand over the mouthpiece.

"I don't think so," I replied.

"Okay, Mr. Robertson, Dawn'll be there," Sunny said into the phone. " 'Bye."

End of conversation. No muss, no fuss.

Eventually Sunny put her board away and we turned to our other favorite topic — food. The W♥KC has a health-food cookbook, and each of us keeps a file of personal recipes that we update all the time.

Maggie was in the middle of describing a scrumptious soba noodle dish, with sesame paste and watercress, when the phone rang again.

"We Love Kids Club!" Sunny announced into the phone. "What? Who *is* this? Get out of here, is this *Ellen*?"

I smiled. Ellen Bliemer is a friend who loves practical jokes. One time she called as a radio DJ and convinced Sunny she'd win a thousand dollars if she named some obscure rock tune.

Sunny's brow became more and more wrinkled. "Uh-huh . . . okay . . . I guess . . . um, can I call you right back?" She rummaged in her night table drawer, took out a pencil and a piece of paper, and scribbled a number. "Got it. 'Bye."

We were staring at her as she hung up. "What was that about?" I asked.

Sunny looked dumbfounded. "She says

she's a feature-story writer from the *Palo City Post* — Ms. Lieb."

"Rhonda Lieb?" Maggie said. "She wrote about my dad once."

"Oh my lord." Sunny's face was turning red. "Maybe it wasn't Ellen."

"What did she want?" Jill asked.

"She said she's writing a series of articles about kids who runs businesses. She heard about the We Love Kids Club and wants to make an appointment to interview us."

"*Whaaaat?*" I squeaked.

"Whoa, let's do it!" Jill said.

"When?" Sunny asked.

"How about tomorrow?" I suggested.

Maggie nodded. "Okay with me."

"Me too," Jill added.

"Try the number she left," I said. "If the newspaper answers, you know she's for real."

Sunny smiled weakly. "You do it. I feel like a total dork for asking if she was Ellen."

Me? Call the biggest local newspaper to arrange an article about the W♥KC? Twist my arm.

Looking at Sunny's scribble, I tapped out the number.

A voice barked, "Positydeskenfeet, murbletch!" (Well, that was what it *sounded* like.)

"Uh, hello? Is this, uh, Ms. Lieb?"

"Rhonda! Line t — "

Silence. I was on hold.

A moment later a much nicer voice said, "Hello, Rhonda Lieb speaking."

"Hi, my name is Dawn Schafer, calling about the We Love Kids Club — "

"Oh, yes, thank you for getting back to me so soon. You . . . sound different."

"Well, the girl you talked to is . . . indisposed right now." (I'd heard that word on TV. I hoped I'd used it right.) "But our club has decided that tomorrow would be all right for the interview."

"Great! About this time? Say, four-thirty?"

"Four-thirty?" I echoed.

Sunny, Maggie, and Jill nodded so fast I felt a draft.

"Okay," I said. Then I gave her Sunny's address.

"Terrific. See you then."

" 'Bye."

The moment I hung up, the room practically exploded.

"We're going to be famous!" Sunny shrieked.

"Where did she hear about us?" Jill asked.

"Is she bringing a photographer?" Maggie wanted to know.

We were higher than three kites. If the phone had rung for a sitting job, I'm sure we wouldn't have heard it. Mrs. Winslow knocked on our door to make sure a bat hadn't flown into the room or something.

The We ♥ Kids Club in the *Palo City Post*? Now *that* was cool.

CHAPTER 3

*D*ing-dong!

It was 4:47 on Wednesday. My friends and I had gathered at Sunny's house. I guess Ms. Lieb was as casual about time as the W♥KC is. She was seventeen minutes late. We had been sitting on the living room sofa for at least half an hour, waiting.

You know how it is when you're on pins and needles for a long time. You get a little punchy.

"She's here!" Sunny screamed.

We all sprang up at once. Maggie's green hair-tail whipped me across the face. Jill, who was eating a whole wheat cracker with cashew butter, chewed furiously and wiped her hands on her white pants.

Sunny reached the door first. She pulled it open and Ms. Lieb breezed in. "Hi! Rhonda Lieb," she said, shaking Sunny's hand. "Sorry for the delay. You must be Sunny."

Ms. Lieb was much younger than I expected. She had short brown hair, a friendly smile, and was wearing a beautiful cotton cardigan over a white T-shirt and gray stirrup slacks. She could have been a college student.

We introduced ourselves nervously. (Well, *Maggie* wasn't nervous. She's had dinner with Keanu Reeves.)

Mrs. Winslow must have heard the commotion, because she came into the room and offered Ms. Lieb some coffee.

In seconds we were sitting around the living room. Ms. Lieb opened her shoulder bag and pulled out a cassette recorder. "Does anyone mind if I tape you?" she asked.

"No," we said.

"Fabulous. Let's get started. The purpose of this series of articles is to spotlight the youthful spirit of enterprise in this area — show the community the *good* things that are happening with our kids. I'm talking to a youth-run car wash, a kids' video company, and a tutoring cooperative. I heard about your group through the principal at the Vista School." She looked at us for a response.

We all kind of grunted positively. Sunny was sitting at the edge of the sofa, looking as if she would fall forward. Jill's legs were crossed tightly to hide the cashew butter stain. Maggie was fiddling with a pencil.

26

Mrs. Winslow laughed as she entered the room with a cup of coffee. "Whoa, what happened? Is she giving you a math quiz?"

That did it. We giggled, and the tension began to lift.

"You know, I used to baby-sit, right up through college," Ms. Lieb said with a smile. "I was studying to be an actress, and one day I took an eight-year-old charge, Rena, to an ice cream shop. In walks this famous director who starts talking to *me*."

"Wow," I said. "Did he give you a part in a movie?"

"No, but he gave Rena one. That was when I decided to become a journalist."

We groaned in sympathy. I liked Ms. Lieb already. She seemed like one of us, only grown-up. Soon she began asking us questions. She especially wanted to know about my bicoastalism, Maggie's Hollywood lifestyle, and our interest in health foods.

We explained how the group was organized (which didn't take long). Then we talked about our experiences. Sunny told her about a charge who insisted on taking a carrot to bed every night. Maggie mentioned a girl who poured bubble bath in the dishwasher. Jill described a baking experience with twins, which ended up as a dough-flinging contest. I gave her a cooking story too, about a neighbor I'd sat for who liked to mix toothpaste with milk and cereal for his dinner.

By the time I'd finished that last story, we were roaring with laughter. Even Ms. Lieb was practically falling off the couch.

At about five-thirty a photographer arrived. He introduced himself as Lance and he was, well, a hunk. He was in his twenties, dressed in black, with dark brown hair pulled back in a ponytail, and the deepest, most luscious eyes I'd ever seen.

"I'd like to catch you all in a variety of shots," he said. "Some candid, some posed."

"Okay!" we cried. I think Lance could have asked us to weed the lawn and we'd have agreed.

We went outside. Clover and Daffodil, the two little girls who live in the neighborhood, were playing with their friends Sara and Ruby. Ms. Lieb easily managed to convince them to pretend they were charges (actually, they all are, every now and then). We posed individually and as a group. We went to Sunny's room and pretended to have a meeting. All the while, Lance kept snapping away. He must have used five rolls of film.

When we finally emerged from the house, a crowd had formed in front. (I guess Clover and Daffodil had spread the word around.)

The crowd parted to let Ms. Lieb and Lance

return to their cars. It was like the Oscars. One kid even held out an autograph book to them, although I'm sure he had no idea who they were.

As for us, well, I noticed most of the good-byes were being directed at Lance.

The article didn't appear for five days. Five long, agonizing days.

Each morning the newspaper arrived with a plop on the front doormat. Each morning I carefully checked the features section. I looked at every headline, every little blurb. I even checked the other sections, in case the article had been misplaced.

But there was no mistaking it that Monday. The headline on top of the features page looked like this:

Palo City ♥'s the We ♥ Kids Club:
The Story of a Baby-Sitting Business
by Rhonda Lieb

Under the headline was a photo of the four of us. Sunny had just hit a beach ball in the air, and was laughing. Maggie and Jill were running after the ball with one of the neighborhood kids. And I was watching nearby.

Near the end of the piece, we appeared again, smiling in a posed group closeup that was labeled with each of our names.

Have you ever seen your name and photo in print, knowing they're going to be seen by thousands of people? It's breathtaking. I actually shivered.

I was never a speed reader, but I must have zipped through the article in about three seconds. Here's how it began:

> Who says you can't have fun while you're working hard? Must have been someone who never met the We ♥ Kids Club.
>
> That's right. We ♥ Kids. The name says it all. It was a love for children that brought Sunny Winslow, Maggie Blume, Jill Henderson, and Dawn Schafer together. And they've become the hottest baby-sitting foursome around. (Come to think of it, what parent could resist hiring caregivers with a group name like theirs?)

The article continued from there, describing us and the club. I was "a silken-haired beauty with a laugh like pealing bells" (hey, *she* wrote it, not me). Sunny was "an aptly named fireball of boundless enthusiasm." Maggie was "savvy, hip, and just this side of *au courant*"

30

(whatever that means), and Jill was "warm and nurturing, the calming force of the group."

I could not believe she was talking about us!

I ran into the kitchen to show Dad and Jeff. Dad's face lit up when he saw the article. "*Heyyy!* My daughter the celebrity!"

"Looks like there's a goober on your face in the bottom picture," was Jeff's comment.

"Ha, ha," I replied. The insult did not bother me one bit. "Be right back!" I flew through the house and out the front door.

A few blocks from our house is a newsstand. I biked to it and bought ten copies of the newspaper. Of course I had to show the article to Mr. Klein, the storekeeper — and he cut out a copy of it to put in his window.

Then I raced home and began writing a letter to the BSC. (I would have called Mary Anne, but it was 10:30 A.M. in Connecticut and she'd already be in school.) I was halfway through the letter when the phone rang.

I knew it would be one of the W♥KC members. "I'll get it!" I shouted, running into the kitchen.

Sure enough, it was Sunny. I could tell by her scream. "Aaauuugghhh! I can't believe it!"

"I know! It's great!" I said. "You . . . you 'aptly named fireball'!"

"Huh?"

I laughed. "That's what the article called you! Didn't you read it?"

"Oh! I wasn't talking about *that*. Dawn, we're going to be TV stars!"

Now it was my turn to say "huh?"

"You know Chuck Raymond, the reporter on the local news? He just called me!"

"Get out of here!"

"I mean it! I'm sitting here eating breakfast, the phone rings, and I answer it with my mouth full of Shredded Wheat. I'm, like, 'Huwwo?' and this voice at the other end says, 'This is Chuck Raymond from WPCN, is Sunny Winslow there?' Well, I nearly choked. I coughed and got this wheat shred stuck up my nose. It was horrible!"

"Oh, my lord, what did he want?"

"He goes, 'Our producer saw the article in the paper this morning and he thinks it would be a good human-interest angle for the nightly news. I wondered if we could bring a crew to your house, say, on Wednesday?' Something like that."

I screamed. I couldn't help it. Dad, who'd been shaving in the bathroom, came running into the kitchen to see if I'd just had an accident. He stared at me, stupefied.

"Did you say yes?" I managed to ask.

"Yes! But I forgot to ask you guys!"

"That's okay! Oh, Sunny, this is *sooooo* exciting!"

Dad was still in the kitchen when we hung up. He's not the type to go crazy over stuff like this, but even his jaw dropped when I told him the news.

Jeff? Well, let's put it this way. I did not hear one joke (or insult) escape his mouth during the rest of the day.

I discovered something on Wednesday. Being a star is boring.

At first it seemed incredibly glamorous. The camera crew was at Sunny's house when the four of us arrived after school. Our neighbors had crowded around to gawk. Workers with headphones and WPCN T-shirts were keeping people away from the lawn. Scratchy conversations squawked out of walkie-talkies left and right. Wires snaked around, held down with silver tape. The crew looked ready to start shooting any minute. Or so I thought.

Mrs. Winslow was out on the sidewalk, talking to Clover, Daffodil, Ruby, and Sara — along with some other kids who had dropped by. As we arrived, the kids cheered and swarmed around us.

"Ready for fame and fortune?" Mrs. Winslow asked with a big smile.

Behind us, a sharp voice called out, "Are you the girls?"

We turned to see a bearded guy with a baseball cap approaching us.

"Uh, yes," Sunny answered.

"Hi, I'm Stu, the A.D.," he said. (That stands for assistant director.) "We're still setting up, so Tina will go inside with you to do makeup and hair, okay?"

A gorgeous red-haired woman appeared behind him, holding a bulging satchel.

"Okay," Sunny squeaked.

We marched inside with Mrs. Winslow and Tina. Twenty minutes later we emerged, looking like movie stars (at least I thought so). The crew was still setting up. The kids were playing on the lawn. Chuck Raymond was nowhere to be seen.

We sat on Sunny's porch and gabbed. And sat and gabbed.

Then we finished gabbing and just sat.

And sat. . . .

The crew set up white sheets on square frames. Then they set up lights on tripods. They argued and moved the white sheets. Then they argued and moved the lights. Then they talked into their headphones.

Honestly, I don't know how real movie actors do it. I was totally drained of energy after an hour of this.

Finally Chuck Raymond showed up with the director, a very tanned, very chic woman named Marisol.

The two of them rounded up the kids and told us to begin playing. "Have some fun!" Marisol said. "Be natural."

Oh, sure. Be natural, with fifty people swarming around, pointing mikes and cameras at you. No problem.

"Playing" never looked so stiff. We W♥KC members were lifeless from the wait, and the kids kept looking into the cameras. One of the boys got bonked on the head with a plastic ball and began to cry. Terrific.

Chuck Raymond, bless his heart, knew just what to do. He's a fantastic mimic, and he put on a little act for us. (I could see Jeff in the crowd, looking at him in awe.) Soon we'd loosened up. Tina rushed over to freshen Mr. Raymond's makeup and put *spray paint* on a bald spot on the back of his head (yes, really). He turned to the camera as we played on the lawn, and began his talk: "Here in Palo City, four extraordinary young women have become the most popular people in the neighborhood. . . ."

He sounded natural, but he was actually reading the words from an electronic screen next to the camera. After a few "takes" of that, we went into the living room, where he interviewed us. Each time anyone said something, it had to be repeated immediately — one time so the camera person could shoot the speaker, and another time to shoot the listener's reaction. (They were going to edit the film to make the interview look like one conversation.)

By the time the crew left, it was pitch-dark outside. All four of our families (including Carol) were now at the Winslows', and we decided to celebrate by going out for an early dinner.

As we headed for the cars, Sunny said, "Dawn, do you realize how long everyone was here today? This is going to take up the whole news broadcast."

"Maybe it'll be, like, a special report," I replied.

For about the twentieth time that day, we squealed and hugged each other.

"Make me barf," Jeff said, plopping into the backseat of Dad's car.

The broadcast was scheduled for Friday night. Carol showed up after dinner with a director's chair for me, tied with red ribbon. The word DAWN was on the back, in the middle of a gold star. A pair of sunglasses and a visor hung from the arms.

I wore them as I made a huge bowl of popcorn. Sunny, Mr. and Mrs. Winslow, Jill, and Maggie came over a half hour before the show, with nuts and granola bars and chips.

We gathered around the TV at showtime. I checked and double-checked the VCR to make sure I'd programmed the tape right (which didn't really matter, because everyone I knew was taping it). Jeff tried to act nonchalant, but he was so excited he couldn't sit still.

"Good evening, and welcome to the eight o'clock news," the anchorwoman said.

My friends and I squirmed and looked at each other. I grabbed Sunny's hand.

Well, we sat through the international news. Then some commercials. Then the national news. Then more commercials. The weather. The sports. *More* commercials. Then . . .

"Now we go to Chuck Raymond, who has the story of a very unusual business, whose customers are, well, some pretty happy parents. Chuck?"

This was it. Our big moment. Now we were *all* clutching hands. Mrs. Winslow was starting to cry.

Chuck Raymond appeared, saying his introductory piece, looking as if he were making up the words. In the background, we were running around and laughing. The way the camera was angled, you couldn't see any wires or white sheets or crew or gawking neighbors.

It looked as though Chuck Raymond had just happened by Sunny's house with a mike in his hand.

"There you are!" Carol exclaimed.

Sunny, Jill, Maggie, and I were silent, eyes wide and mouths open.

The camera cut to the living room — and me, describing the club! I nearly died. I looked so . . . wide. And pale. But I didn't really care. I was on TV!

They cut me off at the end of a sentence. Then Maggie said a few words, Sunny told about a sitting experience, and Jill nodded enthusiastically. A few more outdoor scenes, and it was over.

"That's it?" Jill said.

Maggie looked at her watch. "Four minutes. That's not bad."

A whole, grueling afternoon for four minutes. How weird.

Ah, show biz. At least I now had a *lot* more to include in my letter to the members of the BSC.

Not to mention a videotape to send them.

CHAPTER 4

"**Y**ou look so different!"

Stephie was in awe of my TV performance. She told me she'd fallen asleep during the broadcast, so I brought her the tape when I sat for her on Saturday. She made me play the W♥KC segment five times.

"I look like a ghost," I replied.

Stephie shook her head. "Oh, no. You always look so pretty, Dawn."

I do love Stephie. And not only because she says nice things about me.

Our friendship has really grown. When I first met Stephie, she was this frail little thing with terrible asthma, who always seemed on the verge of crying. Whenever I'd talk to her and try to draw her out, she'd only nod or give one-word answers.

So I decided not to force anything. I just quietly made myself available to her. Little by little she began opening up, and I discovered a sensitive, fun-loving girl. The more I got to know her, the more she reminded me of Mary Anne. (In fact, when my friends in the BSC visited Palo City, Stephie and Mary Anne grew pretty close.)

Like Mary Anne's mom, Stephie's mom died when she was a baby. Stephie has talked about her only once, very matter-of-factly. She said that since she couldn't remember her mom, she didn't feel any sadness. (I wondered if she was telling the truth. Mary Anne doesn't remember her mom, either, but she often cries when she thinks of her.)

A month or so after I started sitting for Stephie, her dad told me her asthma was improving. He was convinced it was because she was happier (Stephie's attacks are usually brought on by emotional stress). Whoa, did that make me feel good.

Now Stephie and I are almost like sisters. She always asks for me to sit for her when Joanna's out.

Our video clip was fading on the TV. "Thank you, Chuck," the TV anchorwoman said with a bright smile. "It's nice to know local parents can leave their kids in good hands."

"Almost makes this bachelor want to go out and start a family," the sports announcer said with a chuckle.

"Oh my, Gary, is that a proposal?" the anchorwoman asked.

They both started laughing. (Ugh.) I reached for the remote.

"She's *single*?" Stephie asked.

"I guess," I said. "But I think those kinds of jokes are, like, written in advance."

"Oh. Too bad. She's so beautiful. Did you get to meet her?"

"No," I said. "Only Chuck Raymond."

"Rats. I wish my dad would date someone like *her*."

Aha, a matchmaker! Yet another side of shy Stephie Robertson. "Well, if I find out anything about her, I'll let you know."

"I like your dad's girlfriend. Wouldn't it be great if they got married? Then you'd have *two* moms."

"Yeah." (To be honest, it didn't sound great at all. It was something I was trying hard not to think about.) "Don't worry. I'm sure your dad will meet someone nice."

She shrugged. "Probably not. He hardly ever goes out anymore."

I shut off the TV. "You really want a mom, don't you?"

Stephie looked at the floor. "I guess. I used to pretend Joanna was my mom, but I don't anymore. It's not the same." She suddenly smiled and stood up. "Want to see something?"

"Sure."

Stephie ran upstairs to her room. I heard a drawer open and close. When she returned, she was clutching a smudged old envelope. She held it out to me and said, "Open it."

I did. Inside was a typical school photo — a bookcase in the background, Stephie looking into the distance, smiling awkwardly with a tooth missing.

It wasn't a great picture. Stephie's dress was old-fashioned, her hair looked weird and stiff, and she seemed heavy.

Then I realized something. Stephie didn't have any missing teeth.

And the date scrawled in the margin was almost thirty years ago.

I gasped. "Stephie, is this. . . . ?"

"My mom," she said. "Doesn't she look like me?"

"Oh, wow. This is incredible!"

Stephie carefully put the photo back in the envelope. "I like to look at it sometimes. I make believe we're talking to each other."

My throat tightened. I could feel tears coming to my eyes.

Stephie ran upstairs to put the photo away. When she came down again, she said she was dying to go outside.

We spent the next hour or so playing catch and riding bikes. Stephie saw a kid do a wheelie, and tried desperately to do one herself.

She couldn't, but I was impressed. She used to hate physical activity.

On our way home, Stephie said to me, "You're fun, Dawn. I wish you'd stay in Palo City for good."

"Oh, Stephie, I wish I could, too. But I'd miss my other family."

"My teacher told us someday people might be able to clone themselves into identical twins. That would be so cool. Then you could be in both places."

"I'll find the laboratory and sign up," I said.

Back at Stephie's house, we ate a big cheese-and-cracker snack. Mr. Robertson was due home in fifteen minutes, so I mentioned to Stephie that I would have to leave pretty soon.

"Can we draw?" Stephie asked.

"Okay," I said.

Stephie found some blank paper and crayons. "Let's draw our families."

"All right."

I used a light green crayon to draw a rough map of the United States. On the right side I drew three people: my mom, Mary Anne, and Richard (Mary Anne's dad). On the left side I drew Jeff and my dad. I couldn't figure out on which side to draw myself, so I finally decided on the top of the map. I drew a blonde girl with hands stretched to both coasts.

Then I looked at the West Coast side and realized I hadn't drawn Carol. I felt guilty. She was *like* family, sort of. I think she and Dad are in love, and she is at the house all the time.

Then I thought, *Nah.* She wasn't related. That had to be the requirement.

I added a surfboard and a bright sun on the West Coast. As I was deciding how to decorate the East Coast, I glanced at Stephie's paper.

With her tongue peeking out of the corner of her mouth, she was busily drawing four people next to a house. I looked closer.

A small female and a tall male were obviously her and her dad. Between them was a woman. I figured that was Joanna.

But on top of the paper, floating in the sky over the three figures, was a second woman. "Who's that?" I asked.

"That's my mom," Stephie said. "In heaven."

I looked again. Her mom's face wore a huge smile, and wings were coming out of her dress.

Then I looked at the other woman, the one between Stephie and her dad. She was wear-

ing a white dress with a funny kind of hat
that drooped over her face.

"Is that Joanna?" I asked.

"No," Stephie said, shaking her head.
"That's what my new mom will look like someday."

I realized what her outfit was.

A wedding dress with a veil.

CHAPTER 5

"**W**ait! One at a time. What was the last name of the people who called you, Jill — Van Druten? How do you spell that?" Sunny was frantically paging through the W♥KC record book. It hadn't been opened in weeks.

Usually, when we *do* use the book, we all just write our own jobs in it. But this time Sunny figured it would be easier if one person handled the scheduling. (This is about as organized as the W♥KC gets.)

"V-A-N, space, D-R-U-T-E-N," Jill replied.

"And yours, Maggie?" Sunny said.

"Smith. S-M-I-T-H."

"Duh. Thanks for the help."

Maggie suddenly let out a gasp. "Oh, *no*! I think I double-booked myself! Is the eighth a Tuesday?"

"Hang on." Sunny closed the address section of the book and turned to the calendar. "No, it's a Monday."

"Whew," Maggie said.

"What are you talking about?" I asked, looking at the calendar on Sunny's wall. "It *is* a Tuesday."

"Nope," Sunny insisted, holding out her book. "Look, Dawn."

I glanced at it. "Uh, that's last year's, Sunny. Look at your wall."

Sunny's eyes widened. "I knew I forgot to get something at the stationery store."

What a meeting. A week had gone by since the TV broadcast. As you can see, things were becoming a lot less laid-back.

If the history of the W♥KC is ever written, I think it'll be divided into two eras: BF and AF. Before Fame and After Fame.

Our phones were ringing day and night. I don't know *how* some of these people found our numbers. Maggie received a call from a parent in San Diego (I guess because she's the only Blume in our county's phone directory). Maggie had to explain patiently that Palo City was more than two hours away. I received a call from a very young-sounding boy who wanted me to send him my autograph. Sunny was grilled by an eighth-grade girl who wanted to start *her* version of the club in another town. Not to mention all the actual baby-sitting jobs that came in.

Neither the Palo City Press nor WPCN had

publicized our phone numbers (for privacy reasons) but they received tons of calls asking about us.

Great, huh? Well, yes and no.

I'd always thought of the Baby-sitters Club as a tight ship, and the We ♥ Kids Club as sort of a surfboard riding the waves. Each was fun in its own way.

Now I realized the W♥KC was in danger of wiping out.

Sunny yanked the calendar off the wall. "This will be our official calendar until I get a book-sized one," she said. "Okay, let's start again, one by one. Tell me who called, and the date and time you're supposed to sit. Dawn?"

I was holding four scraps of paper in my hand, on which I'd written the information. "Let's see, I said I'd sit for Stephie on Thursday . . . two new kids, Sarah and Nathaniel Walden, a week from Friday . . . a girl named Catya McMullen next Saturday . . . Erick and Ryan DeWitt on . . . oh, *no*!"

Thursday, I had scribbled. The same day I'd agreed to sit for Stephie.

"I double-booked, too!" I said. (Me, veteran BSC member, of all people! I imagined Kristy wagging a finger at me.)

"Wait! Wait! Wait!" Sunny said, writing furiously. "What day was Catya — "

Bleeeeep!

I picked up the phone. "We Love Kids Club!"

"Hello, my name is Lisa Schwartz, and I saw your article in the paper," a voice said. "We just moved into town, and we're wondering if you have a brochure."

A brochure? "Uh, no, we don't as of yet," I said, "but one of us will be happy to meet with you and your children."

"Well, I need someone this Friday. I'd love it if one of you could come a half hour early and meet my two boys."

"The Facklers called you?" I heard Sunny suddenly say to Jill. "They called me, too!"

Mrs. Schwartz heard her, too. "Is this a bad time?" she asked.

"No, not at all," I lied. "Let me take your number and call you back in a few minutes."

I wrote the number down, hung up, and plunged back into the roaring surf.

Sunny told me the current problem. Not only had Maggie and I both double-booked sitting jobs, but somehow Mr. and Mrs. Fackler had double-booked two different *sitters!*

"What a mess," I said.

Sunny let out a big sigh. "Let's solve one thing at a time. What should we do first?"

"I guess I could call Mr. Robertson and the DeWitts," I said, "and see if I can sit for the kids together."

"I'll do that, too," Maggie agreed.

"I bet the Facklers will call one of us when they realize what they did," Jill said to Sunny. "Then the one who gets the call can call the other."

"What if they don't call?" Sunny asked. "And if they do, which one of us should take the job?"

Jill shrugged. "We could both go, and split the money."

Okay, that was it. I had had enough. It was time for us to paddle to shore and build a ship.

Or at least a nice, sturdy raft.

"I hate to say it," I began, "but maybe we should talk about making rules. I know we're different from the Baby-sitters Club, but things are getting out of hand."

I'd had this conversation once before with Sunny. She had insisted that the W♥KC didn't need to be as rigid as the BSC. Up till now, she'd been right. We'd never had as many clients as the BSC did. But that was obviously changing.

I expected everyone to protest. Instead, they just looked at me.

"What should we do?" Jill asked.

"Well, first of all we should decide on regular meetings," I said. "Then we make some fliers to pass around and post in public places — fliers that say parents should only call during meeting times, and use Sunny's phone number. This way we can easily record our jobs. That's how the BSC works. We also have officers, so nobody gets confused about who does what."

"I don't like the idea of *officers*," Maggie complained. "Like, 'Aye-aye, Captain Sunny.' That seems so official."

"We don't *have* to do everything exactly the same as the Baby-sitters Club, Maggie," Jill replied. "Maybe just *some* things."

"Or we can make up our own rules," Sunny suggested. "Stuff that makes sense for us."

Maggie shrugged. "As long as we can be kind of loose about it. No attendance sheets or demerits or secret handshakes and stuff."

Sunny's eyes lit up. "Ooh, secret handshakes! I *like* that idea!"

"Me too!" Jill said.

For the next few minutes, we tried out different We ♥ Kids Club handshakes — behind our backs, under our legs, jumping in the air. Finally we collapsed from laughter.

By the end of our meeting, we hadn't decided on any changes. But we did agree that *something* had to be done.

For the time being, we'd just try to cope.

And buy a new calendar.

CHAPTER 6

Hurray! A ☆ is born! And to
Monday
think, we knew you before you
laughed like pealing bells! Will you
still remember us at the Oscars?

Seriously, I am so proud of you,
Dawn. Claudia got your package
Friday, and she called us right away.
We had a special meeting at four
o'clock. Thanks for sending all those
copies of the article. Claudia gave
a dramatic reading of it, especially
the great description of you. Then
we watched the video about ten times.

Janine hooked up a second VCR
and made a tape for each of us,
so when I got home I watched it
some more. Now I know it by heart.

We do have one problem, though. I think Kristy is a little jealous, and her Idea Machine is going wild . . . .

Did I tell you that Kristy is a complicated person? Well, she is.

Ninety-nine out of a hundred Kristy ideas are fantastic. But there's always that one clinker.

From Stacey's letter, I could tell that Kristy had really outclinked herself.

It started at that Friday BSC meeting. Everyone went crazy over the article and the video. Even Claudia's sister, Janine, watched it. (Janine's comment was "very good production values.")

Afterward the members of the BSC retreated to Claudia's room.

"This is so cool!" Stacey kept saying.

"I think Dawn's telegenic," Shannon said.

"You believe in that stuff?" Claudia asked.

"Huh?" Shannon looked at her blankly.

"Reading minds and everything?"

Shannon threw back her head and laughed. "That's tele*path*ic! Telegenic is like 'photogenic on television.' "

Then Kristy spoke up. "*We* should make a video."

"That would be great," Jessi piped up. "We could do a takeoff! Daddy does an excellent TV announcer impression — "

"No, I mean *really* make one," Kristy interrupted. "Hey, if the We Love Kids Club could be on TV — "

"Kristy," Stacey said, "you don't just *make* a video and put it on TV. The news station contacted the We Love Kids Club. No one's contacted us."

"Well, why not?" Kristy snapped. "We've been around longer than the We Love Kids Club. If it weren't for us, they wouldn't exist!"

"Okay, so they were lucky," Stacey replied. "Maybe someday we'll be lucky, too."

Fortunately the phone started ringing with sitting jobs before Kristy could answer Stacey. It was past five-thirty. Kristy was so worked up, she'd forgotten to call the meeting to order. (I believe that is a first in BSC history.)

I should explain something. As I mentioned before, Kristy and Mary Anne are best friends. They grew up as next-door neighbors and started playing together when they were still in diapers.

When I moved to Stoneybrook, *whoosh*, all of a sudden Mary Anne became my best friend, too, and then moved into my house and became my sister. You can imagine how Kristy felt. I was not her favorite person. Fortunately things smoothed out over time. Kristy and I became friends and stayed friends. But a little germ of tension never quite went away.

I guess the germ started to grow again when Kristy saw the article and video. (At least that was Stacey's opinion.) There I was on TV. First I'd "stolen" Kristy's best friend, then taken her greatest idea to a bunch of girls who got it all wrong, and now *they* (and I) were getting all the glory.

By Friday the germ had become a raging flu.

That night Kristy baby-sat for her younger brother (David Michael), her stepsiblings (Karen and Andrew), and her adopted sister (Emily). After she put them to bed, she read the article and watched the video again.

I can just see the wheels turning in her head. I'm sure she *tried* to put aside her feelings about me. I'm sure she thought she was just cooking up another idea to help the Baby-sitters Club.

Whatever was on her mind, here's what she decided: If the TV stations and newspapers weren't coming to her, she would go to them.

The next morning, Saturday, she decided to "pitch" a story about the Baby-sitters Club to the news. ("Pitch" means "try to sell an idea." Kristy had heard that term on TV and liked it, probably because it sounded like baseball.)

She began making phone calls. The first one was to the *Stoneybrook News*.

"*News* switchboard, may I help you?" an operator asked.

"Hello, my name is Kristy Thomas and I'd like to speak to the person in charge of, um, like, publicity for — "

"Please hold," the operator interrupted. (I *hate* when that happens.)

Click . . . rriiiing! "Children's calendar, weddings, and obituaries," a voice said.

Well it took awhile for Kristy to reach the right department. When she did, the response was, "We're all booked with features for awhile. Have you tried your school paper?"

That wasn't the response she wanted — so she tried the Stamford newspaper (Stamford is the nearest city to Stoneybrook). They were even less interested.

Next Kristy tried the two local television stations. The first one wouldn't let her past the operator.

She tried a different tactic for the Hartford station. She actually wrote a script for her "pitch."

Somehow she got through to a station official. As soon as she heard the woman's voice,

Kristy barged ahead, trying to read her script in an adult voice: "Hello, this is Kristy Thomas of the Thomas Talent Agency, and I have exclusive rights to the story of an extraordinary organization known by every parent in the Southwestern Connecticut radius. It's called the Baby-sitters Club."

Kristy took a deep breath. The woman said, "The what?"

"The Baby-sitters Club."

The woman burst out laughing. "Is this some kind of joke?"

"No!" Kristy shot back. Then she remembered her mature voice: "I mean, imagine, an answer to the age-old problem of parents everywhere — "

"Do you have a tape?"

"A tape?"

"If you represent this act, or whatever it is, you must have a tape."

Kristy hadn't figured that into her script. "Uh, well, I'll have to . . . call you back."

Ball four. Kristy had to return to the pitcher's mound.

One thing about Kristy, she never gives up. She couldn't wait to bring up her big plan at the Monday BSC meeting. She figured everyone would be excited about the idea. Maybe they could make a tape of their own and send it to the station.

As soon as the meeting began, she reenacted her pitch. The reaction? Total silence.

"So, what do you think?" Kristy said. "Should we make a tape?"

Claudia and Stacey shared a Look. So did Shannon and Jessi. And Mary Anne and the floor.

Finally Stacey spoke up. "I don't remember deciding we were going to contact the media."

"Sure we did!" Kristy protested. "Remember on Friday when we said we never got on TV or in the papers — "

"Well, yeah, but we didn't say anything about actually *trying*," Stacey said.

Kristy shrugged. "What's so terrible about trying?"

"Kristy, you're the one who's always lecturing us about group decisions," Claudia said. "You went and did this without telling us first."

"But — but — " Kristy sputtered, "I didn't think anyone would mind something like this!"

"Remember when Mary Anne got her hair cut?" Stacey asked. "We felt a little hurt because she hadn't told us in advance that she was going to do that."

"Well, that was dumb of us," Kristy replied. "We all agreed."

"But this isn't," Shannon piped up. "I

mean, why do we need *more* publicity, Kristy? Dawn's in California, Mallory's home recovering from mono, and calls are coming in like crazy. We can barely keep up with the jobs as it is."

"I just got a call from Dawn," Mary Anne said. "It sounds like the We Love Kids Club is going crazy."

"That's because they're not organized!" Kristy exclaimed. "They're hardly even a club."

"Look," Stacey interrupted. "We said we didn't want to take in new members to replace Dawn and Mal, right? If we get any more publicity, we'll have to recruit half of SMS."

"We could hold our meetings in the gym," Claudia suggested.

"You'd have to order M&M's by the truckload," Stacey said.

"Oh, that reminds me!" Claudia cried. "Get off the bed."

Mary Anne jumped off and Claudia reached under the mattress to pull out a huge bag of Reese's Pieces. "Food break!"

"I thought the bed felt a little lumpy," Mary Anne remarked.

Jessi laughed. "Mary Anne Spier, the Princess and the Pieces."

Everyone groaned. The meeting was finally returning to normal. Sort of.

Kristy grabbed a fistful of candy and munched away, but she was glowering. She hardly said a word the rest of the meeting.

Reading about this incident made me feel a little guilty. Maybe I should never have sent that article and video.

Oh, well. At the end of Stacey's letter, she promised she'd keep me posted on the "Kristy Crisis."

CHAPTER 7

Thursday was my double-sitting day.

I was lucky. Mr. Robertson and Mrs. DeWitt were nice as could be when I explained what had happened. They agreed I could take Stephie over to the DeWitts' and sit for all three kids there. Erick (who's eight) and Ryan (six) were happy she was coming over.

Stephie, on the other hand, did not seem thrilled with the idea.

She barely said hello when I picked her up. And she was silent practically as we walked to the DeWitts'.

Finally I said, "Stephie, are you mad about something?"

"Yes. I *hate* Erick and Ryan."

"But I thought you didn't know them very well."

Stephie looked at me as if I'd said the stupidest thing in the world. "They go to my school, Dawn. And they're cootie heads."

"What makes you say that?"

"It's just true." She stared at the ground and pouted. "And I know why we're going there. You *forgot* you were sitting for me, so you said you'd sit for *them*. And you said we were like sisters. Sisters don't forget!"

No wonder she was upset. I stopped walking and crouched down next to her. "Oh, Stephie, I just made a mistake. You wouldn't believe how many phone calls I got after the We Love Kids Club was on TV. It was all so confusing, I couldn't think straight. I promise it will never happen again."

"I wish that TV show had never happened," Stephie said under her breath.

"Hey, you want to know a secret? When I went to your school, sometimes we wrote 'CP' on our palms."

She gave me a baffled look. "Why?"

"It stands for Cootie Protection. Just in case. Here, give me your hands."

She did. I took out a pen and wrote a tiny "CP" on each palm. "There," I said, "now you can't catch cooties."

A teeny smile appeared on her face. "Are we still like sisters?"

"Of course."

She looked admiringly at her CPs. "Well . . . okay."

Whew. Stephie remained in a pretty good mood — until we reached the DeWitts' front lawn.

There, dueling with plastic swords, were Peter Pan and Captain Hook.

"Blast you, Pan! I'll cleave you to the biscuit!" Ryan shouted.

"*Brisket*, dummy!" Erick replied.

Ryan lowered his sword. "Uh-uh. No such word."

Erick lunged forward and whacked Ryan's sword away. "You're a codfish, Hook!"

"Hey, no fair!" Ryan protested.

Erick finally glanced our way. "Look! There's Wendy and Tiger Lily."

Stephie was glaring at them. I could tell she had no intention of being Tiger Lily.

Fortunately the front door opened just then, and out walked Mrs. DeWitt. "Hi, Dawn! And hello, Stephie. Oh, look at you. Just as pretty as always!"

Mrs. DeWitt is tall and thin, with huge brown eyes and a wonderful smile. She's an actress and has been in tons of commercials.

Ryan, who had disappeared behind the house, now returned with a long rope. "Erick, you tie up Tiger Lily and I'll rescue her."

Stephie looked horrified.

"Ryan Martin DeWitt, you put that rope

away!" Mrs. DeWitt ordered. She smiled at Stephie and added, "They're just excited to see you."

Stephie stayed glued to my side while Mrs. DeWitt quickly gave me some instructions. Then she looked at her watch and said, "I have to run. Have a good time. I left a snack inside for you and the kids."

"Snacktime!" Erick shouted. "Yea!"

"First come say good-bye." Mrs. DeWitt knelt down and the boys ran into her arms, almost knocking her over.

"Will you be back in time to tuck us in?" Ryan asked.

"Way before that, sweetheart," she said, kissing his forehead. "And so will Daddy." She wrapped them both in a huge hug. "Be good."

The boys ran inside.

As Mrs. DeWitt headed to her car, Stephie called out, " 'Bye," with a wave of her hand.

" 'Bye, honey," Mrs. DeWitt replied. "Have fun."

Stephie beamed. I could tell she liked Mrs. DeWitt.

Now if only she could feel that way about her sons.

We walked inside. The DeWitts' living room was crammed with photos — baby pictures of Erick and Ryan and their proud, smiling parents; a younger Mrs. DeWitt on stage, taking a bouquet of roses from Erick, in his dad's arms; the four of them on a mountain hike, at the zoo, on a ski slope, and so on.

Stephie stopped to look at every one, her mouth open in awe.

In the kitchen, Erick and Ryan were wolfing down cream cheese-and-jelly sandwiches. With their free hands, they were reaching into a bag of Cheez Doodles.

"Hey, you're taking mine!" Ryan shouted.

"There's plenty left," Erick shot back, grabbing a fistful of Doodles. "It's a free country."

"Give me those!"

Ryan reached across the table, knocking the remaining Doodles to the floor.

"Dawn, look what Ryan did," Erick said in a singsong voice.

"You tattletale!"

"She saw you!"

I sighed. Eventually the mess was cleared away and we finished our snacks peacefully.

Then Erick decided he'd try to make friends with Stephie. "You want to play Turtles?" he asked. "I'll be Leo and you be Raph."

"And I'm Don," Ryan added.

Stephie shook her head. "Uh-uh."

"Okay," Erick said. "Um . . . how about hide and seek?"

"I don't want to play that either."

"Freeze tag?"

Stephie shook her head. "I can't play anything rough. I might get an asthma attack."

"Oh." Erick looked at her blankly.

"Come on, Leo," Ryan said. "*Cowabunga,* dude!"

The boys ran outside, off to . . . wherever Ninja Turtles go.

Now, Stephie's asthma no longer prevents her from running around. And anyway, it's usually emotional stress that triggers her attacks. Come to think of it, though, maybe running around with Erick and Ryan could be classified as emotional stress. So I wasn't about to drag Stephie outside. But I couldn't just ignore the DeWitt boys.

In a pile of stuff by the back door, I saw two Skatch paddles and a ball. "I know," I said. "We can play Skatch outside, just you and me."

Her eyes lit up. "Okay!"

That worked terrifically — for about ten minutes. Then Erick insisted on playing. Before long, he and Ryan were trying to prove who could throw the fastest.

Well, when two boys have a throwing contest, you know what happens. Someone always gets beaned on the head.

And you can guess who it was.

"Owwwww!" Stephie cried.

"It's only rubber," Erick said.

"Do we have to take her to the hostipal?" Ryan asked.

"*Hospital*, stupid!"

"I'm not stupid!"

"Whoa, chill out, guys!" I said.

Stephie was hugging me, whimpering.

Ryan walked closer to her, staring at her head. "Does she have a big bump?"

Immediately Stephie stuck her palm in front of his face.

Ryan's eyes widened. "*Cootie protection?* I don't have cooties!"

"Yes, you do," Stephie said.

Erick was rolling on the ground, laughing. "Ryan has cooties!"

As for me, I was vowing to myself never, *ever* to double-book again.

It seemed like weeks before Mrs. DeWitt returned. I don't know who was happier to see her, the boys or me.

We were in the den when she bustled through the front door, carrying a large paper bag. "Anybody home?"

Erick, Ryan, and Stephie all sprang to their feet. "Mom!" the boys screamed.

"What's in the bag?" Erick asked.

"Just some odds and ends for you guys."

She set it down on the coffee table and started unloading it. "Socks, shoelaces, chewing gum . . ."

"Oooh, gum!" Erick squealed.

As he happily distributed the gum, I gave Mrs. DeWitt a report on the afternoon. Out of the corner of my eye, I saw Stephie examining the shoelaces. She was fingering them as if they were jewelry.

That seemed kind of strange, until I looked at her sneakers. Her own laces were dirty, frayed, and full of knots.

A few moments later, we exchanged good-byes, and Stephie and I left. For the first few blocks, she didn't say a word. Finally I asked, "Stephie, what's on your mind?"

"Mrs. DeWitt should be *my* mom, not theirs!" she blurted out. "Then I would always get snacks and nice stuff, too."

"Joanna makes you snacks," I said. "And you could ask her or your dad to buy you some new laces."

Stephie nodded. "I know *that*. But if I had a mom, I wouldn't have to ask. She'd just buy them."

I sighed. I really love Stephie, and I'm glad that I've been able to do so much to help her.

But finding a mom was one area in which I was totally helpless.

CHAPTER 8

Thursday had not been an easy day. I wanted so badly to relax, and just have a quiet family evening.

So what was sitting in the driveway when I got home? Carol's red Miata.

Big deal, I told myself. So the house would be a little loud. So Carol would want to know every detail about my day. So she'd laugh hysterically at Jeff's dumb jokes. It was okay. She had every right to be there. She was Dad's girlfriend. And I shouldn't be mean. After all, she *had* bought me that director's chair and the sunglasses and visor.

So why did I feel like heading right back to Stephie's?

Of course I didn't do it. I put on a smile and walked inside.

Dad and Carol and Jeff were all in the living room. Standing.

Dad was still wearing his suit and tie. Carol

was wearing a dress, with a big, colorful beret in her red hair — and makeup, which is very unusual for her.

Behind them, I could see Mrs. Bruen busily putting a meal on the dining room table. It looked like Thai food, which I love. Four places were set, with all our best china.

I looked on the bright side. At least we weren't having vegetable *chimichangas* again.

Jeff was about to burst with excitement. "Dad's going to make an announcement!" he said.

Oh, good, I thought. The last time something like this happened, I was in sixth grade and Dad had gotten a big promotion. (It was one of the last times I saw Mom and Dad happy together.)

"What's the news?" I asked.

A smile spread across Dad's face. He turned toward Carol. She grabbed his arm and planted a kiss on his cheek. "Go ahead, honey," she said. "You tell them."

I didn't like the sound of this.

"Well, Dawn, Jeff," Dad said. "You're about to have a stepmother."

I froze. The words floated around in my brain, falling apart into strange syllables. For a moment I thought I'd heard wrong. Or I hadn't quite grasped the meaning.

"Dad and Carol are getting married!" Jeff shouted.

Thank you, Jeff. Now it was crystal clear.

And so was the huge diamond on Carol's new ring.

I could see Mrs. Bruen watching me, looking for my reaction. Along with everyone else. I suddenly felt as if a giant magnifying glass had been placed in front of me, and they all were peering through it.

I did the only thing I could do.

I bolted.

Between Jeff and Mrs. Bruen, through the dining room, through the kitchen, down the hall, and into my room.

I slammed the door behind me.

My feet would not stop moving. I paced back and forth. I wanted to scream but my teeth were locked together.

This was wrong, wrong, wrong. They couldn't just decide like this. Not without at least *mentioning* it to me first. How long had they been planning this? Why did they keep it such a big secret from Jeff and me?

How dare they?

I decided to let them know how I felt. If I had to yell and scream and throw Thai food, I would make sure they knew how serious this was.

I grabbed the doorknob and yanked open the door.

The first thing I heard was Mrs. Bruen's voice. "Poor dear. Is she all right?"

"Ohhhh, she's angry," Carol said, sounding shocked and hurt.

"No, not Dawn," Dad reassured her. "Not about this."

"Maybe she just wanted to change into something nice," Jeff suggested.

I took a deep breath. What was I doing? Was the announcement really that surprising? Jeff and I both thought Dad might marry Carol. We'd talked about it. Dad had even dropped hints a couple of times.

Even *Stephie* and I had discussed it.

Still, hearing the news for real came as a shock. But I had to admit, that wasn't *their* fault. And it was not fair of me to storm away and ruin everyone's celebration.

You have no idea how hard it was to pull myself together. But I unclenched my teeth and walked back down the hall.

Dad and Carol studied me with these shaky little smiles. Jeff was standing by the table, drooling over the food. Mrs. Bruen was puttering around in the kitchen.

"Is everything okay?" Dad asked me, trying to sound cheerful.

Up, lips! I commanded. I felt my face trying

to smile. "Yeah. I was just . . . taken by surprise, that's all. Boy, that's big news!"

Carol looked relieved. "Well, let's sit down." She angled her head toward the kitchen and said loudly enough for Mrs. Bruen to hear, "Everything smells soooo fabulous!"

We gathered around the table and stood stiffly for a moment. I wondered if there were rules about this — who sits first at an engagement-announcement dinner?

Well, correct or not, Jeff made the first move. He plopped into his chair and spooned some curried noodles onto his plate. "Come on, I'm starving," he said.

The rest of us sat down. Dad produced a bottle of champagne and poured some for each of us (a very small amount for Jeff and me). Then he stood up and raised his glass high. "To the most beautiful family in the world — and its newest member."

"Hear, hear! There, there!" Jeff the Stand-up Comic cheered.

No, no, I wanted to say. But I didn't. I raised my glass and took a tiny sip.

Jeff gulped his down. "Yechh!" he said, breaking into a fit of coughing. Carol bolted up from her chair and began pounding him on the back.

"Ow! Stop!" Jeff protested.

"It's okay, Carol," Dad said with a smile.

"As long as he's coughing he's all right."

Carol looked embarrassed. "I guess I have some things to learn about being a mother, huh?"

No comment.

Soon Jeff stopped coughing, and we ate. Well, three of us did. Carol seemed too excited. She talked instead. Nonstop.

Okay, maybe I'm exaggerating. But she had barely touched her plate by the time the rest of us were helping ourselves to seconds.

"So your dad tells me to dress up because we were going to a *basketball game*. Imagine! I mean, why *dress up* for that? So he picks me up, drives toward the stadium, and says, 'Let's get some coffee first.' He pulls up to this sweet little cafe — and the game's supposed to start in ten minutes. Well, little do I know he's going to propose. And on his knees! *Everyone* in the cafe is watching, and when I say yes, they start applauding, and the waiters break into song. It was so romantic. Oh, was I blushing!"

"I would have gone to the game," Jeff remarked.

"Did you show them the ring?" Dad asked Carol.

She held out her hand. The diamond was surrounded by sapphires. "Isn't it *breathtaking*?" she said.

I, for one, was still breathing. "Beautiful," I replied.

Jeff glanced at it and shoved some shrimp with peanut sauce into his mouth.

Now that Carol was quiet for a moment, I decided to ask, "When's the wedding?"

"The sooner the better!" Carol said.

"We haven't decided," Dad added.

So there was still time!

Stop that, I said to myself. I couldn't believe how negative I was being. Dad looked happy, and that was the most important thing. Wasn't it?

Carol picked up her fork and began eating again. The rest of us were using chopsticks, even Jeff. We always did. It was a family tradition. I remembered how much fun we had learning to use them. Eating Thai food with a fork seemed, well, unnatural.

I tried to ignore that. It wasn't a big deal.

Then Jeff reached for some coriander chicken and knocked his glass of water on the floor. "Uh-oh," he said.

Carol shot out of her chair. She ran into the kitchen and returned with a fistful of paper towels. "No problem," she said. She began wadding up the paper and trying to soak the water out of the carpet.

Well, first of all, Jeff is old enough to clean up after himself. Second, it is so environmentally wasteful to use paper towels for a water spill. A dry sponge would have soaked it up just fine.

But no one seemed to mind. Dad and Jeff thanked her, and Carol marched proudly back to the kitchen to throw out her soggy portion of destroyed American forest.

After dinner, as we cleared the plates, Jeff asked, "What's for dessert?"

Carol and Dad shared a glance, and I knew something was up.

"You kids get strawberry shortcake," Dad said, "but your stepmom and I are going out to celebrate."

"*Again?*" Jeff said.

"Oh, sweetie," Carol said with a laugh, "it's not often a person gets engaged, you know."

Stepmom? Sweetie? I guess I was going to have to get used to some new words around the house.

And it looked as if I'd also have to get used to seeing less of my dad.

He and Carol left, laughing and chatting, arms around each other. I sat at the kitchen table with Jeff and ate about three strawberries.

"Full, huh?" Jeff asked.

"Yeah," I replied, standing up. "Excuse me. I've got lots of homework."

"There's no excuse for *you*!"

"Can it, Jeff," I snapped.

I cleared my plate, went straight to my room, and plopped on my bed.

I had tried my hardest. I had been polite and friendly. I hadn't ruined the celebration.

But now what? Now Dad was getting married. Carol was going to be eating every meal with us. I'd be seeing her first thing in the morning, and she'd probably be kissing Jeff and me before bed each night. She'd go shopping with us and take vacations with us.

And when I wanted to have a nice, quiet talk with Dad, Carol would be there.

I realized something then. I hated her. There was no use pretending otherwise. Who did she think she was, barging in on our lives? She was a loud, obnoxious, teenage wannabe, and she didn't deserve someone like my father.

Then again, it took two to make an engagement.

My teeth were clenching again. This wasn't what I'd had in mind when I came to live in California. I'd had to leave my other family, upset my friends, work hard to adjust to a new school — and for what? To spend six months with *Dad*. Couldn't he at least have waited until I went back to Connecticut? I guess he *preferred* to spend time with her.

One thing seemed clear. I wasn't wanted here.

But I *was* wanted somewhere else, by my mom and my stepsister and my best friends.

That was when I made my big decision. I was going to move back to Stoneybrook.

CHAPTER 9

"Jeff Schafer, get back in this house," I heard my dad call out.

"I can walk to school by myself!" Jeff retorted. "I'm *ten!*"

"No you're not, you're Jeff." (Ooh, two points for Dad!) "And I'm your father, who makes the rules around here. *Dawn! Are you almost ready?*"

"Just a second!" I shouted back.

In my room, I scribbled furiously on a sheet of stationery. It was Friday, the morning after the wedding announcement. I had a little announcement of my own to make.

I wasn't going to make it aloud, and I certainly wasn't going to wait for dinner. By dinnertime I hoped to be high above the country, flying eastward.

Quickly I glanced over my note:

Dear Dad,
 *I won't be home from
school because I'm on my
way to Stoneybrook. But
I'm sure you don't mind.
Now you can spend as
much time as you want
with your future wife.
You won't have a daughter
around to cramp your style.
 Good luck with your
wedding plans. Tell Jeff
I still love him. And
don't be upset. I'll be
with people who care
about me.*
                Love, Dawn

It sounds sneaky, I know. But I had no choice. Can you imagine if I'd *asked* permission to cut school and fly to Connecticut? My mom would think I was crazy. As it was, getting her to let me leave Stoneybrook in midyear had been like moving a boulder up a steep mountain.

Once I arrived in Stoneybrook, I'd explain what had happened, and she'd accept it. I was sure she would. I did have a home there, after all.

I folded up the note, put it in an envelope, and stuffed it deep into my backpack.

Then I put on the pack and grabbed the pen and another sheet of paper. Quickly I tiptoed into Dad's empty bedroom. His credit cards were strewn on the top of his dresser. I copied the number of one card onto the paper and shoved it into my pants pocket.

Boy, did I feel guilty about that. But it wasn't as if I were *stealing* Dad's money. He was going to have to pay for my flight back eventually, right?

I was ready.

My heart was beating like crazy. If I pulled this off, it would be a miracle.

I ran into the kitchen. Dad was standing at the table — tying his tie, drinking his coffee, and reading the morning paper at the same time.

Probably thinking about Carol, too.

"Sorry I took so long," I said, "but I wanted to clean up because today is Mrs. Bruen's day off . . . isn't it?"

Dad glanced up for a minute and furrowed his brow in thought. "Friday . . . you're right, it is."

Good. I'd just wanted to make sure. Now my plan was set!

Phase One: The Preparation. Walk to school as if nothing were wrong.

"Well, 'bye, Dad!" I called out.

"So long, Sunshine!" he replied.

Sunshine. Ugh. I wondered what nickname he was going to give Carol. Motormouth?

Jeff pushed open the front door. "Come on, *Sunslime*."

"You're so funny I forgot to laugh," I answered. I couldn't be too mad at him, though. This was the last we'd be seeing of each other for awhile. Obnoxious as he was, I was going to miss Jeff.

Halfway to school, Jeff left me to walk with some friends. I felt a tug inside. He was going to be so *mad* at me for leaving unexpectedly. I wanted to give him a big hug and a kiss good-bye, but not in front of his friends. He'd never let me forget it.

Eventually I met up with Sunny and Maggie. I was *dying* to tell them my secret. But I couldn't. It would be too painful to see their reactions.

As we approached school, Sunny and Maggie were laughing about my description of Thursday's sitting job. And looking into their faces, I began to have cold feet. Would they forgive me? How could the W♥KC possibly survive now with only three members?

I thought about staying. Then I imagined what it would be like to come home from school and be greeted at the door by Carol.

That was all it took. I was ready for Phase Two of my plan: Dawn's Acting Audition.

I stopped walking. "Ugh, my stomach."

"Are you okay?" Sunny asked.

"Yeah." I walked a few more steps, then grimaced. "Owww, what a cramp. Must have been the shrimp omelet I ate this morning."

Shrimp omelet? I don't know how I thought of that. But it worked. Sunny and Maggie both nodded.

"Dawn, you do *not* belong in school today," Maggie said.

Sunny took my arm. "I'll walk you home."

Uh-oh. That wasn't part of the plan. "No, you'll be late. I can make it fine."

"Are you sure?" Maggie asked.

"Uh-huh. I just need to lie down. I'll . . . see you later."

"Okay. . . ." Sunny said reluctantly.

"We'll tell your homeroom teacher, so don't worry," Maggie assured me.

"Thanks," I replied. " 'Bye!"

"Feel better!"

I felt *awful* lying to them. As soon as they were out of sight, I checked my watch. It was eight-thirty, and Dad would be rushing out of the house.

By the time I reached our house, his car was gone. I let myself in the front door.

Phase Three: The Getaway.

I dropped my bag and pulled the credit card number out of my pocket. Then I went to the kitchen and riffled through the Yellow Pages.

Being bicoastal, I know all the airlines that fly to Connecticut. I began calling them.

I was on the phone for half an hour (mostly on hold). The first airline I reached had a seat on Tuesday. The second was booked solid for the next week.

But the operator at the third one said, "I'm showing a cancellation for two seats, but it's a three o'clock flight this afternoon. And it leaves from LAX, not John Wayne. Is that all right?"

John Wayne Airport is close to our house. LAX is Los Angeles International Airport, which is almost an hour away.

"Fine!" I cried. "I'll take one seat."

I read her my dad's credit card number. Then she mentioned the price.

I almost fainted.

But hey, if I left a few months later the flight might cost *more*. Prices tend to go up over time, so I was actually doing Dad a favor.

At least that was what I told myself.

I wrote down the information and hung up. Then I pulled my good-bye note out of my backpack and added a couple of lines:

P.S. My flight arrives in Connecticut at 11:00 tonight, their time. I'll call Mom from the airport.

'Bye!

I left the note on the kitchen table. Then I raced into my room, grabbed a shoulder bag from my closet, and began to pack.

It didn't take long. I wouldn't be needing my light California outfits in Stoneybrook. I'd left all my heavy winter clothes there, anyway.

I made sure to take my journal, a few photos of Jeff and Dad, and my copies of the W♥KC article and video. I stuffed every last penny of my baby-sitting money into my pocket.

At nine forty-five I looked through the Yellow Pages again and called a cab. When it arrived, I raced outside as fast as I could, wearing a wide-brimmed hat. (The last thing I needed was for some neighbor to see me and call my dad.)

I climbed in, slammed the door, and ducked below the window. The driver pulled away, and Phase Four began: Dawn's Trip Home.

You would not believe how much it costs to take a cab from Palo City to Los Angeles. I nearly died.

Almost all of my baby-sitting money went into that ride. I had enough left to buy one bag of nuts, which had to last me for three and a half hours while I waited for my flight.

But that was okay. I wouldn't need any money on the plane. And afterward I'd be in Connecticut!

I kept thinking I saw familiar faces in the airport. I was petrified someone would recognize me. Under my wide hat, I began to feel like an international spy. A young guy on his way to Cleveland sat next to me for awhile. When he asked my name, I told him it was Mariso Van Raymond. I even tried to use an exotic accent.

At two forty-five I boarded. For the first hour of the flight, I could barely sit still. I wanted to scream out my secret to everybody — I, Dawn Schafer, had left school, booked my own flight, and taken a cab to L.A. By myself.

And it was so *easy*. I've never felt so independent in my life.

My exhilaration lasted until dinner. Somewhere over Nebraska, reality began to set in.

Maybe it was the wilted salad, or the tasteless roll. Or the fact that there weren't any vegetarian meals left so I had to share my flight with part of an overcooked chicken carcass.

Whatever it was, dread started creeping

through me. It was about 5:30, California time, and Dad would be coming home. I imagined his and Jeff's expressions when they saw the note. Then I pictured how Sunny and the other girls would react when they found out.

They would feel horrified. Disappointed. Betrayed.

What had I done? I'd never dreamed of cutting school to go to the *movies*, let alone to board a cross-country jet and charge it to my dad. It was insane.

Suddenly, two thousand miles away, I felt pretty stupid.

I was a criminal. I was a runaway. I had stolen money from my own father. I would step off the plane into a circle of policemen with handcuffs. Rhonda Lieb would call me "the W♥KC fugitive" in the paper. Chuck Raymond would interview Sunny, who'd hardly be able to speak through her tears.

My eyes began to close over Indiana, and I slept too deeply for my worries to turn into nightmares.

I woke up to the sound of the flight captain saying, "We are now beginning the descent to our final destination. The weather in Connecticut is cold and clear, about twenty-eight degrees. There's a fresh coat of snow on the ground, but the runway is completely dry."

Snow! I'd almost forgotten what that was

like. I began to feel excited again. Soon I'd be hugging Mary Anne. We'd stay up all night talking. I'd wake her tomorrow morning to build a snowman.

I was fluttery all over as the plane landed. I rushed to the exit. As I neared the end of the ramp, I scanned the terminal for a pay phone.

But I didn't need one. Mom was waiting for me at the gate.

And her expression could have burned a hole through sheet metal.

CHAPTER 10

Saturday

Dear Dawn,

It seems silly to be writing this to you now. I mean, we just spent the whole day together talking. (Well, most of the day.) I'm so sorry about what happened.

I hope things aren't going too terribly right now. I've thought a lot about your problem. I can imagine how you feel. I mean, it

*was hard for me
when my dad got
married, even though
I liked your mom
so much.*

*Anyway, don't worry.
We all love you. I
just thought you
should know that....*

I got Mary Anne's letter on Wednesday. It was so nice to see some sympathetic words for a change. The weather may have been in the 70s and 80s, but it sure felt frosty in my dad's house.

Yes, I was back in Palo City. Needless to say, my trip to Stoneybrook did not work out. (Boy, is *that* an understatement.)

Let me start from the beginning. First of all, I was shocked when I saw Mom at the airport. I wanted to run to her and hug her, but the look on her face stopped me.

"Hi!" I said. "How did you know I was coming?"

The Mask of Doom opened her mouth. "How do you think I knew? Your father called me two hours ago."

"Oh," I said. "He found the note."

"Yes, he did. And he was in a panic. He spent an hour on the phone calling every airline on the West Coast. Then he thought you might have hitchhiked to the airport, so he contacted the police. When he called me, he could barely speak. I could hear Jeff in the background, crying."

I could tell Mom was trying very hard not to scream at me. Her head looked as though it were vibrating. I'd never seen her like this.

"Sorry," I said, gazing at the floor.

"You'd better be. How could you have done this, Dawn Schafer? How could you be so irresponsible and immature? Not to mention *deceitful*. Do you *know* what you put your family through? After all we did so you could move to California for six months, all the adjustments we made, all the emotional strain? And you just up and booked a flight on your father's credit card for the fun of it? What on Earth could have possessed you to do something like this?"

Tears welled up in my eyes. "It wasn't . . . for the fun of it," I managed to say.

Mom pointed to a nearby chair. "I brought your coat. Put it on while I call your dad to let him know you got here safely. He's worried sick, and he feels responsible. We'll talk more on the way home."

My down coat was lying on the chair. That

was a good sign. At least Mom wasn't going to let me freeze.

I watched my mother make her call on a pay phone. I could hear Dad's voice booming from the other end. He did not sound happy. Fortunately Mom didn't make me speak to him.

Then she and I walked silently to the parking lot and found her car. Neither of us said a word until we were on the highway, heading home.

I tried to explain my feelings about Carol and Dad. As the words came out of my mouth, they sounded shallow and stupid.

But Mom listened carefully. She hadn't known about the engagement, and I think the news shook her up a little, too. Slowly the smoke coming from her ears began to clear away.

"Did you tell Dad how you felt?" she asked.

"No," I said. "I was too angry."

"So you ran away from the situation."

"I guess."

"Here's what I don't understand, Dawn. You honestly thought we wouldn't mind? You thought you could just change your plans and it would affect nobody but yourself?"

"Mom, I — I just wasn't thinking about all of that. I was upset."

"I can see that. But now quite a few people

are upset. Including your dad. You're going to have a lot to work out with him. Starting with that plane ticket."

"I'll pay him back out of my baby-sitting money, I promise. No matter how long it takes. Everyone in the BSC has told me they're incredibly busy."

"Sweetheart, it's going to take longer than you think. First of all, you're going to have to repay him for *two* tickets. And second of all, you're going to be doing it in California."

I stared at her. *"What?"*

"I booked a flight back for you. It leaves tomorrow afternoon at four o'clock. Don't forget, you still have some time left on your six months, Dawn."

"But — but — don't you want me to stay?"

Mom sighed. Her voice softened. "Of course I do. But not under these conditions. If you're ready to come home, you need to make a plan that includes us all."

I slumped into my seat. Part of me understood what she was saying. I shouldn't have been so selfish. But nobody was seeing *my* point of view. First Dad had crowded me out of his life, and now Mom was sending me away, too. (Funny how she got worked up over the ticket I'd charged, but it was no problem spending the money to send me back.) Wasn't I important to *anybody*?

We arrived home after midnight. Richard and Mary Anne had already fallen asleep. I crept upstairs to my room.

Everything was just as I'd left it. It looked so comfortable and homey. As I threw my backpack on my bed, I noticed a folded-up note there.

I picked it up and read:

Dear Dawn,
If I fell asleep before you got home, I'm sorry. I'm sure you've been yelled at enough by now, so I won't ask questions like why did you do it. I'm just glad tomorrow is Saturday so we can actually talk to each other in person! We might as well make the most of our few hours together, huh?

Welcome home.
Love, your
sister,
Mary Anne

It was the nicest thing I'd seen all day. Leave it to Mary Anne. For the first time since I'd gotten off the plane, my mixed-up feelings came pouring out. Anger at Carol, anger *and* love for Dad, love for Mary Anne, hurt at my mother's reaction, shame for what I'd done . . . they were all so powerful and bewildering.

I buried my face in my pillow and cried my heart out.

The next thing I knew, someone was knocking on my door.

I struggled to open my eyes. It was light outside. My night table clock said 7:09. But my watch said 4:09, and so did my California-conditioned body.

"Come in," I croaked.

The door burst open. "Hi!"

Mary Anne ran in and jumped on my bed. She was still wearing her L.L. Bean nightgown, but she looked refreshed and excited.

Me? I felt as if I'd been run over by a steam-roller, but boy, was it good to see Mary Anne.

"I know, I'm not supposed to be nice to you," she said. "But I am soooooo happy you're home!"

I sat up and gave her a hug. Both of us burst into tears.

Over Mary Anne's shoulder, I saw Mom peering into the room. She was trying to look stern, but I could detect a trace of a smile. "Dawn," she said, "Richard's making break-fast downstairs. You and Mary Anne can hang around the house until your flight, but you are not to call any of your friends while you're here. Is that understood?"

I nodded.

As soon as Mom left, Mary Anne pulled away from me, found a tissue, and blew her nose. Then she drew in a deep breath and said, "Tell me *everything*!"

So I did. At least I tried to. Our conversation bounced all over the place.

At one point Mary Anne mentioned the Kristy crisis. "Did you get my letter about Kristy's latest scheme?"

"Well, I know she called the TV station — "

"She went further than that. I couldn't believe it. We had all decided we didn't need more publicity. But in one of our meetings — just one — we didn't get any calls from clients.

We started joking about how we *should* try to get on TV."

"And Kristy didn't think it was a joke," I guessed.

"Mm-hm. She actually sent her copy of the We Love Kids Club video to the TV station. She enclosed a letter that said something like, 'They were big in California, but they're even better in Connecticut!' The problem was, she forgot to rewind the tape. So the TV people put it on and saw a commercial for indestructible pantyhose."

"No!"

"Yes. They thanked Kristy and sent back the tape with a list of advertising fees."

We cracked up.

Well, Mary Anne and I gabbed while we got dressed, gabbed over breakfast, and didn't stop gabbing all day.

The afternoon rolled around much faster than I had expected. Mom drove me back to the airport. Our ride there was almost as grim as the one home had been the night before.

We did hug and kiss good-bye, though. And Mom had tears in her eyes when I left.

The flight took off on time, and I braced myself for what would happen when I saw Dad.

And Carol.

CHAPTER 11

Ohio hadn't changed. Neither had Kansas. Nor Minnesota. In fact, the country looked exactly the same as it had the day before.

Fortunately I didn't have to deal with a lump of dead flesh in my meal on the return flight. *This* airline had a reasonable meatless lasagna.

It didn't matter. I had no appetite. Besides, I might have a second chance later. For all I knew, Dad had another ticket back to Connecticut lined up for me. I could see myself becoming a human tennis ball, going back and forth, back and forth across the country. Maybe I could rack up enough Frequent Flyer miles to take a free trip to China. Then neither Mom nor Dad would have to see me.

Dad was waiting at the airport. I noticed he did not have a ticket in his hand (whew). But he did have the same disgusted and angry expression on his face that Mom had had.

And he was ready with most of the same words, too. Once again I heard *selfish*, *immature*, and *irresponsible*. I had to give Dad points for originality, though. He also came up with *underhanded*, *spoiled*, and *reckless*.

Then came the ritual of driving home. I wasn't looking forward to that. My flight had come into LAX again, and it was going to be a long ride to Palo City.

But Dad surprised me. After he finished his lecture, he said, "Dawn, I know something is bothering you terribly. And I am your father. If you need to tell me anything, I'm all ears."

"You mean, you're not angry?" I asked.

"I didn't say *that!*" Dad scowled, but then he actually broke into a smile.

Hallelujah. I felt as if I'd emerged from a swamp and into the sunlight.

"Well, to tell you the truth," (I took a deep breath), "this has to do with you and Carol."

Dad exhaled. "I can't say I'm surprised. Go on."

I told him how I felt about Carol. I listed her habits that bothered me. I mentioned how hurt I'd felt when they'd announced their engagement.

Dad listened intently. After I finished, he shook his head and said, "I had no idea,

Dawn. I thought you and Carol had worked out your problems. Why didn't you tell me things had gone off track?"

"She's your *girlfriend*, Dad. I didn't want to hurt your feelings. Besides, she's not a bad person. And you seemed to be happy with her. I *was* trying hard to like her. But when I realized she was going to marry you and become my stepmom, everything just exploded, I guess."

"So you thought I'd betrayed you, and you wanted to get back at me."

"No, I thought you didn't want me around."

"Oh, Sunshine, how could you think that? You know that's not true."

"It turned out *Mom* was the one who didn't want me," I said, staring out the window. "She had bought my return ticket before I'd even landed. Boy, was I stupid."

"It wasn't that she didn't want you, Dawn. She's dying for you to go back to Connecticut. But she and I both feel you need to learn to live up to your commitments. Moving out here was a big decision, not something you can change on a whim."

For about the tenth time in twenty-four hours, I was getting choked up. "Okay," I murmured.

Dad gave me a quick glance, then turned

back to the road. When he spoke, his voice was gentle. "Being a divorced kid isn't easy, is it?"

"Nope," was the only word I could manage, between sniffles.

It was about 7:15, California time, when we arrived home. As we pulled into the driveway, Jeff ran out of the house.

"Hi, Dawn!" he said. "Are you okay?"

"Yes," I replied.

"How did you *do* it? Like, buying the ticket and going to the airport and all? That is so cool!"

"Don't even *think* about it!" Dad called from the driver's seat.

Jeff and I walked to the front door together. "Did you do it because of Dad and Carol?" he asked.

I nodded.

"I don't blame you," he whispered. "If you had told me, I would have gone with you."

I smiled at my brother. I was glad to see the real Jeff emerge from behind the joke machine for a change.

As we walked inside, Mrs. Bruen ran to me and gave me a big hug. "Welcome home, honey," she said.

More waterworks.

Eventually I went to my room, followed by

my brother. I could tell he'd been afraid, and he didn't want to let me out of his sight.

He shut the door behind him and plopped on my bed. "Dawn," he said, his voice barely audible, "did Dad tell you about his argument with Carol?"

"No." I sat down next to him. "What happened?"

"Well, she came over last night when Dad was screaming at Mom on the phone. So she and I played seven games of checkers, and I won five. When Dad got off the phone he told Carol what you had done. She said, 'I'll stay and help,' and Dad said, 'No, I think you'd better go home,' and Carol got all upset. She said, 'If I go home I'll just worry. Please, I'm going to be part of the family, remember?' He said, 'Yes, I remember, but that's not the point now. This is something important that I need to work out with Dawn and her mother.' And she said, 'I know, I know, there'll always be something more important than me.' Whoa, did Dad blow up! He called her selfish."

That sounded familiar.

"And she *cried*," Jeff went on. "And you know what else? On the way out, she threw her engagement ring on the floor."

"So it's off?"

Jeff looked puzzled. "Yeah, I said she *threw* it."

"No, I mean the engagement."

"Nahhh, they talked on the phone later, and it sounded like the fight was over. But Dad has to repair the ring."

Wow. I had never seen Dad and Carol angry with one another. Maybe their relationship wasn't perfect after all.

Later on, when I was alone in my room, I heard Carol come in the front door. She and Dad talked for a few minutes. Then I heard a knock on my door.

"Mind if I come in?" Carol's voice said.

"No," I replied.

She stepped in, looking concerned. As she shut the door behind her, she said, "I'm glad you're back. Are you too tired to have a little talk?"

I felt completely talked out. I wanted to tell her to come back the next day.

But if I turned her away, Dad would probably be angry, and that was the last thing I wanted.

Besides, I was feeling guilty. I'd dumped on Carol, but she wasn't the real reason for my anger. I had been feeling rejected by Dad. He could have gotten engaged to *anybody*, and I'd probably have felt the same way.

"I'm not too tired," I said.

Carol sat down on the bed. She was smiling,

but she looked stiff and nervous. "So, how was . . . your flight?"

I didn't want to beat around the bush. "Carol, I'm sorry about what I did. This is supposed to be a happy time for you and Dad, and I'm spoiling it for you."

"I was worried that — " She shifted uncomfortably. "You know, that you didn't want us to get married."

"Don't worry about that, Carol. The problem has more to do with me. I really am glad you and Dad are engaged. I mean, it did come as a shock, and I didn't exactly know what to say. Or how to act." I looked her in the eye and tried to smile. "But I know how happy my dad is. He really loves you."

Carol's eyes filled. She opened her arms and we shared a hug.

The last thing she said before she left was, "Friends?"

I forced a smile. "Yeah. Friends."

I went to bed immediately afterward, but I was too exhausted to fall asleep right away. For a few minutes I just lay there, relieved that the talk with Carol was over. Maybe now I could put my nightmare behind me, prepare for the wedding, and work like crazy to pay back those plane tickets.

Which meant I'd be baby-sitting until I was ninety.

CHAPTER 12

Saturday

Dear Dawn,
   Hi! I got your letter today while Jessi
and I were baby-sitting.
   *Mal's allowed to
sit again. She's
still a little
weak, but she's
almost totally
better.*
   Dawn, I CAN'T BELIEVE YOU WERE
ACTUALLY IN THE SAME TOWN AS US!
   *You should
have called.*
   Stop, Jessi! (She's kidding, Dawn.)
Anyway, we laughed at the part of the
letter about Jeff — how he's been calling
you names all this time, and then he cried
after you'd left.

105

It was as if
you were describing
our sitting job.
Whew. After today I may have to
go back to bed. . . .

Mallory was up and around now, but her
parents weren't letting her participate in after-
school activities or go on sitting jobs. But she
could go to school and baby-sit at her own
house — as long as she took it easy.

Unfortunately, taking it easy and sitting for
the Pikes is like keeping dry in the shower.
Impossible.

As I mentioned before, Mal has *seven*
younger siblings. The oldest are ten-year-old
triplets named Adam, Jordan, and Byron.
Then there's Vanessa (who's nine); Nicky
(eight); Margo (seven); and Claire (five).

It takes at least two to sit for the Pikes,
usually one BSC member plus Mallory. Lately,
though, two seems too few: The triplets have
decided they are old enough now to do whatever they want.

On that dreary winter Saturday, they were
making a secret potion in the basement. Vanessa the Dragon was hiding from Claire the

Knight, and Margo and Nicky were playing checkers in the living room.

Jessi and Mal were in the kitchen, making lunch.

"Where is she?" Claire asked, rushing into the kitchen. She was brandishing a toy ray gun and wearing a cape made from an old shirt.

"I thought you were a knight," Jessi said, looking at the gun.

"A space knight, you silly-billy-goo-goo," Claire answered.

Oh. Of course.

Claire disappeared upstairs and into a bedroom.

"RAAAUUUUUURRRGHHHH!" Vanessa was a pretty convincing dragon.

"Aaaaaaugh!" Claire ran back into the kitchen, giggling, with Vanessa in pursuit.

"You woke me up behind the bed. Now I shall eat your little head!" Vanessa howled. (She loves to speak in rhymes. It drives everyone crazy.)

From the living room, Margo yelled, "I win again!"

"But I didn't move yet!" Nicky protested.

"You can't, doofus," Margo replied. "You're trapped! New game!"

"I hate this!" Nicky said.

"EEEEEWWWWWWWW!" floated up from

the basement, followed by wild laughter.

Jessi and Mal exchanged a Look. "I'll go this time," Mal said with a sigh.

She trudged downstairs. "Okay, guys, what are you doing?"

The boys were clustered around a big sink next to Mr. Pike's workbench. "Get out!" Adam said.

Mal ignored him. She moved closer and saw a pail in the sink. Inside the pail was a disgusting brown liquid — and the Pikes' hamster, Frodo, sloshing around in total confusion.

"What *is* this?" Mallory asked.

"It's a formula," Jordan said.

"We're making a secret growth serum and we want to see if it works," Byron added. "But Frodo won't drink it."

On a nearby counter, Mal could see a small carton of milk, a bag of potting soil, some marshmallow Fluff, butterscotch syrup, baking powder, wadded-up lint from the clothes dryer, a pile of sawdust, and some Elmer's glue. The secret ingredients.

"You guys, this is ridiculous," Mal said. "Get Frodo out of there and wash him off."

Adam shook his head and exhaled. "You're getting in the way of science!"

"It's all right," Jordan said. He didn't drink any of the potion, but he's covered with it. I

108

think that'll work. We can put him in the cage and monitor his growth."

The boys began arguing over who would have to lift the poor animal out, and Mal went back upstairs. She bumped into Nicky, who was on his way down. "Can I play?" he asked his brothers.

"No!" they shouted at once. Adam added, "You have to be ten to join the science club."

"Do not!" Nicky yelled. "You started it when you were nine."

"At least we don't have bad breath!" Byron shot back.

"Byron!" exclaimed Mallory.

"It's true!" Adam said. "He smells like sardines."

"I *like* sardines!" Nicky protested.

"Ewww," moaned the creators of the growth serum.

Nicky stormed upstairs.

Mal returned to lunch duty. Before long, she and Jessi had put together a pile of sandwiches, and they called the other kids into the kitchen.

You should see lunch at Mallory's house. It's not exactly elegant dining. Kristy calls it "Pikes at Trough."

The kids scarfed down their lunch in seconds. Afterward the triplets went into the hallway and began putting on their coats.

"Uh, where are you guys going?" Jessi asked.

"To Carle Playground," Adam replied.

"Hmmm, did they ask *you* for permission, Jessi?" Mal inquired.

"Nope," Jessi answered innocently. "Did they ask you?"

The triplets looked at each other and rolled their eyes. "Can we go?" Byron grunted.

"It is cold and yucky out, and it looks like rain or snow," Mal said.

"So?" Jordan replied. "We're not going *forever*."

"I'll go with you," Nicky volunteered.

"Oh, great," Byron muttered.

"No way, Nicky-Nicky-breath-so-icky," Adam chanted.

"*Adam!*" Mallory exclaimed.

"He always gets in the way," Jordan said.

"I do not!" Nicky snapped, his eyes brimming with tears.

"Besides, he might think the fish in the pond are sardines and eat them!" Jordan cracked up at his own joke.

"Come on, we're out of here," Adam said as they headed for the door.

Nicky ran after them, his face bright red. He held the door open and yelled, "Good riddance! I didn't want to play with you barf-heads anyway!"

He slammed the door and ran back through the kitchen. Mal and Jessi felt awful for him. "Nicky?" Mal said.

"I wish they were *dead*!" was Nicky's reply.

"Be careful what you wish for, it might come true!" Vanessa called from inside the living room.

"Good!" Nicky ran to his room and slammed *that* door.

Mal waited a moment, then climbed the stairs and knocked gently on the door. "Are you okay?"

"I'm *soooo* happy they are gone," he said. "I hope they never come back."

"Well, if you need to talk, I'll be downstairs with Jessi."

Nicky murmured something, and Mal went back to the kitchen, where she and Jessi were cleaning up.

Apparently Nicky recovered. A few minutes later he'd sneaked down to the living room and was whooping about how he was going to "demolish" Vanessa at checkers.

About a half hour later, at 1:00, it began to rain. "Ha!" Nicky's voice floated in from the living room. "Now they're going to get wet and freeze!"

The rain fell harder. The house became so

dark that Jessi and Mal had to turn lights on. Then the wind began rattling the windows. Eventually Nicky wandered into the kitchen. "Are they back yet?" he asked.

"Nope," Jessi replied.

Mal looked at the stove clock, which said 1:37. "Hmm, they've been out there awhile. I hope they're okay."

Nicky's brow was furrowed. "Maybe something happened to them."

"Nah, they can take care of themselves," Mal said.

Nicky left, then returned a moment later. "How cold does it have to be to get frostbite?" he asked.

"Cold enough to snow, I think," Jessi replied. "Why?"

"They didn't take their waterproof gloves."

Mal raised her eyebrows. "Are you *concerned* about your brothers, Nicky?"

"No way!"

Five minutes later thunder began to boom. "Uh-oh, where are they?" Mallory murmured.

Nicky ran into the kitchen, looking worried. "Let's call the police," he suggested. "What if, like, a tree fell on them, or they got hit by lightning?"

Mal sighed. "They should know it's dangerous to be out in weather like this."

"Yeah!" Nicky was on the verge of tears now.

"I could go look for them," Jessi said.

Nicky ran to get his coat. "I'll go with you!"

Whack!

The back door slammed open. Adam, Byron, and Jordan tumbled inside. They were panting and laughing, out of breath, and their footsteps made loud squishy noises on the floor.

"Made it!" Adam said.

The boys were sopping wet from head to toe. Their coats and shoes were two shades darker than before, and their hair was matted against their heads.

"What happened?" Mal demanded.

"We tried to come back when the rain started, but it was too heavy," Adam said, "so we went inside the toolshed at the park, to wait it out. But the storm just got worse, so we ran for it!"

"It was *great!*" Jordan said with a laugh.

Mal and Jessi were relieved. Nicky? Well, he hugged and kissed them and told them how much he'd worried.

Just kidding.

His concerned look had already twisted into a sneer. "You're *ten*, and you're too stupid to come in out of the rain?" he said.

"Go wash your head in bubblegum," Adam replied.

"You look like *you* already did, grease head!" Nicky snapped.

"Baby!" Byron said.

"Three Stooges!"

Ah, brotherly love.

CHAPTER 13

"Mm, great sesame noodles," Dad said. "Pass the soy sauce."

Carol quietly passed it, chewing on her sauteed vegetables.

The table fell silent. I could hear the bean sprouts crunching between my molars.

"Knock-knock!" Jeff called out.

"Who's there?" Dad asked.

"Yeah."

"Yeah who?"

"What are you so happy about? *Get it?*"

I groaned. Dad laughed. Carol smiled and ate some more vegetables.

Silence again. My stomach growled. I felt as if we were eating dinner in a library.

For the first time in my life, I hoped Jeff would tell another dumb joke. He seemed to be the only one who wasn't tense.

The house hadn't been the same, since I'd

returned from Stoneybrook. Dad wasn't his usual happy-go-lucky self. One morning he went into a fit when a shoelace broke. Another time he shattered a coffee pot trying to jam it in the dishwasher, then walked off in a huff.

Things were worse when Carol came over. True, she no longer went overboard trying to be cool and talk like a teenager. Now she was going overboard in the *other* direction. She hardly ever spoke. She'd sit at the dinner table looking nervously at Dad and me like a kid waiting to be punished in the principal's office.

She was driving me crazy.

And it was all my fault. The more I thought about it, the more childish and ridiculous my plane trip seemed. If I had just bothered to *talk* to Dad, I would have realized he wasn't rejecting me. But Dad and I were not the only ones affected by my trip. How would *I* have felt if I were Carol, and my fiancé's daughter had run away from home after I'd announced my engagement? Awful. I would *never* forget it.

Despite our talk, I knew Carol wouldn't, either. She couldn't walk into the house without feeling unwanted.

Which did not make for lively dinners, that's for sure.

Explaining my trip to my friends was no

picnic, either. I spent an entire W♥KC meeting doing it. Sunny, Maggie, and Jill were all sympathetic, but I could tell they couldn't *quite* understand it. Maggie seemed annoyed that I'd faked sickness on the way to school that fateful day. The other girls just kept looking at me as if I'd gone slightly looney.

Mainly, though, I think they were relieved that I was back. Jobs were still coming in like crazy, and they couldn't afford to lose a member.

By the way, Sunny *had* bought a new calendar in time for that meeting. Unfortunately it didn't help much. By the time we finished talking about me, it was dinnertime.

Calls kept coming in to all our numbers. Sunny ended up double-booking herself again. She called me in a panic, and I agreed to take one of her jobs, sitting for Erick and Ryan at four-thirty on a Tuesday afternoon. That same day, though, I was already hired to walk Stephie home from school and sit for her until Joanna came back from the dentist. But Joanna had assured me she'd be back by 3:45, so it seemed okay.

Stephie was thrilled when I showed up outside her school that day. She held my hand and we swung arms, walking through the playground. "Dawn, I wrote a story today. I'm going to make it into a book. I'm going to illustrate it, too. And you know who I'm going to dedicate it to? *You!*"

"Oh, Stephie. That's so sweet," I said.

"Hi, Stephie!" a girl called from behind us.

We turned to see a pretty black-haired girl walking toward us with her mom. "Hi, Becky," Stephie replied.

"Who's that?" Becky asked, pointing to me.

Stephie hugged my arm and said, "That's my mommy."

"Is not," Becky said.

Her mom winked at me. "That's the youngest-looking mom *I've* ever seen. What's your secret?"

She and I laughed, talked a bit, and said good-bye. On the way home, Stephie and I passed a corner store. "Ooh, can I get a treat?" she asked. "Please?"

"Stephie . . ."

"Then you won't have to make me an after-school snack."

She had a point. I was going to have to leave just a few minutes after I reached her house. "Oh, all right," I said. "But nothing too sweet."

"Yea! I love when you buy me things, Dawn."

I bought her a bag of chips and we walked home contentedly.

We arrived there at three-thirty. As soon as

118

we were inside, Stephie insisted on showing me her story. I unfolded it and read:

The Special Flower
by Stephanie Robertson

Once upon a time there was a very special flower in front of a wite house. A prety girl lived in there, and one day she was very sad. She ran outside, crying, "Boohoo" She layed down next to the flower.

The flower said "Why are you crying" and the girl said "Because I dont have a mommy. She's dead."

But the flower just smiled. "Go to sleep and dont you wury. I am your mommy."

Well, the girl got angry. She said "No your not! your a flower. My mommy was berried in the ground!"

But the flower just smiled again. "your right,"

she said, "but what ever
is planted in the ground
grows into something
beautifull, doesn't it?"
 The girl smiled back at
the flower. And you know
what? She was never sad
again.
                The End!

"Stephie, that's so . . . moving," I said.

It was, too. I could barely keep from "cryng"
myself.

Stephie said, "The flower's name is Dawn."

Whoa. I didn't know what to say to *that*.
Fortunately Stephie ran into the playroom with
her story then. "I'm going to start illustrating."

Well, 3:45 came and went. I began to feel
nervous. At 4:05 the phone rang.

I picked up the receiver. "Hello, Robertson
residence!"

"Hurro, dhaw?" said a weird, thick voice.

"Hello?"

"Icksh Showah-uh."

I figured it was a crank call, and I was about
to hang up. Then I remembered Joanna was
at the dentist. The last time my dad had gone
to the dentist, he could barely move his mouth

afterward. "Is this Joanna?" I asked.

"Uh-huh! Uh-huh!"

"Um, are you calling to say you'll be late?"

"Uh-huh!"

"Are you finished there?"

"Uh-huh!"

"So I'll see you soon?"

"Uh-huh!"

"Okay, thanks! 'Bye!"

Oh, boy. At my fastest, I'd need ten minutes or so to get to the DeWitts'. I began pacing. I wished Sunny hadn't double-booked herself. I vowed to organize the We ♥ Kids Club somehow.

Joanna arrived at 4:14 and gestured for me to leave. As I bustled out the door, Stephie ran into the front room, looking crushed. "Do you *have* to go baby-sit for those cootie heads?" she said. "I want to show you my illustrations."

"Sorry, Stephie," I replied. "I'll come over tomorrow, okay?"

"Yeah. 'Bye."

Oh, did I feel rotten.

At least I had plenty to think about on my run to the DeWitts'. Did Stephie really want *me*, or did she just want someone to be her mommy? Funny, she wouldn't mind sharing her dad if he were to get married, but she had a hard time sharing me.

I had to admit, I knew how she felt. I sure hadn't wanted to share my dad with Carol. And I completely screwed up my personal life to prove it.

Stephie was lucky, in a way. She was too young to let her jealousy make her do something seriously stupid, the way I had.

Then my thinking shifted. (Maybe all the running had shaken something loose in my brain.) *Ease up, Schafer*, I told myself. I was acting as if I'd committed the worst crime in the world. I wasn't the only person who ever felt jealous. Other people did dumb things, too, and it was easy to forgive them.

I thought of Kristy trying to get the BSC on TV. I don't know if she'll *ever* recover from the fact that the W♥KC "made it" first. I don't know if she'll ever get over her resentment of me. But I love her anyway.

Come to think of it, Jeff could be an unbelievable pain to me, and I still love him. And if Nicky Pike could still have feelings for those three monsters in his house . . .

It's all so mixed up. You resent people you love (like Nicky and his brothers), you love people who resent you (me and Kristy), you resent people who love people you love (me and Carol), you resent not having someone to love (Stephie and her imaginary mom), and you think people who love you resent you (me and Dad, or me and Mom).

Feelings are weird. I don't think I'll ever completely understand them.

As I approached the DeWitts' house, with three minutes to spare, I slowed to a walk. I wanted a glass of water. But even more, I wanted to be with Mary Anne. She knows a lot about feelings. She'd be able to explain things to me.

Suddenly I felt very homesick.

CHAPTER 14

Okay, no more Ms. Nice Girl. I was ready to take action, this time for real. The We ♥ Kids Club *had* to change.

I reached my limit when Sunny called me Tuesday night. She had gone to her sitting job, the one she had double-booked. She'd been in a great mood, knowing that I'd bailed her out.

Unfortunately, she had forgotten to confirm with Mrs. Walsh, the mother of her charge. Mrs. Walsh, thinking Sunny was over-booked and that she had no sitter, had canceled the meeting she was supposed to go to. A very important meeting, judging from how angry she was with Sunny.

This was not good for business. I called a special club meeting. I asked the girls to meet at Sunny's house at exactly ten o'clock Saturday morning. That would give us plenty of time to discuss our future. I told them that the meeting would start promptly, no matter how many of us were there.

Shades of Kristy Thomas. I *never* thought I'd hear myself bossing people around like that.

It worked, though. Everyone arrived by 9:55. And everyone started talking at once.

"Mrs. Walsh chewed my ear off," Sunny reported. "She told me she would never call any of us again."

"Mr. Fackler told me we ought to be more organized," Maggie said.

"He should talk," Jill replied. "He and his wife can't decide who should make the appointments."

"Doesn't his voice sound familiar?" Sunny said. "Like Mr. Ed, the talking horse?"

I was not going to let us get off track again. "Excuse me!" I interrupted. "Let's make a list of our problems, okay? Then, when we finish, we'll make a list of possible solutions."

My friends nodded, as if they'd just heard Abraham Lincoln speak. I took a sheet of paper from Sunny's desk and drew a line down the middle.

"Okay, problems?" I asked.

Sunny: "Double-booking."

Maggie: "Who controls the record book?"

Jill: "We don't know who's doing what job."

Maggie: "Parents have to make too many calls if one of us isn't home, or has already booked a job."

Sunny: "My mom accepted a job for me when I wasn't there, the night before a big test."

I scribbled furiously. Then I said, "Solutions?"

The room became absolutely silent.

"What about regular meeting times?" I asked.

Jill complained that that sounded too rigid. Maggie said it would be a hassle to call all our clients and tell them about the change. To that, Sunny remarked we might not *have* any more clients if Mrs. Walsh told her friends what had happened.

We talked and talked. Finally we settled on a plan:

1. We would have regular meeting times. Every week. (But no guilt trips about lateness.)

2. We would divide up our clients and each notify several of them that they had to call Sunny's number during meeting hours.

3. We would use the record book and check it before confirming a job.

But that was it. We decided not to assign officers or keep a club notebook. Which was all right. Deciding on *any* rules was a major step with this group.

By the end of the meeting we were pretty pleased with ourselves. The We ♥ Kids Club would still be relaxed and fun.

Just a lot more efficient.

I was dying to tell Stephie. She'd be thrilled to hear that double-booking was a thing of the past. Besides, I wanted her to know that I still had time for her, even though things had been crazy lately.

As I walked to her house, I felt better than I had in a long time. And not only because of the W♥KC. It had been two weeks since my plane trip, and the atmosphere in my house was lightening. Carol had actually kept up a fair noise level the last time she'd been over.

I had never thought I'd be happy about *that*.

Stephie answered when I knocked at her door. *"Dawn!"* she exclaimed, her face breaking into a huge grin. "What are you doing here?"

"I just dropped by to say hi and tell you some good news," I answered.

I described our meeting. Stephie's reaction was not exactly what I'd expected. She shook her head and said, "I can't believe you girls are thirteen and you just thought of that."

Before I could reply, she ran inside, calling, "I have to show you my book!"

She returned a few moments later with a

small stack of looseleaf paper, folded in half and stapled together.

The cover showed a drawing of a little girl asleep on the ground. A huge, smiling flower with arms was cradling her.

The flower had long blonde hair.

"That's me, isn't it?" I asked softly.

Stephie giggled. "It's not you, silly. It *looks* like you, and it's *named* after you. But it's just part of a *story*!"

I couldn't help laughing. Poor, sad little Stephie? She was going to be all right.

When I returned to my house, I called Mary Anne.

"Hi!" she said. "How are you? Did you have that big meeting you were telling me about?"

"Yes," I replied. "And you won't believe what happened."

"Good news or bad?"

"Good."

"Great! Wait a minute, Dawn. Kristy's over. I want her to hear."

She called Kristy, who ran upstairs and picked up the other phone. I told them what had happened in great detail.

I was sure Kristy would disapprove. After all, we weren't adopting *all* of the BSC rules. But you know what she said? "I think you're on the right track."

"I mean, we'll never be as organized as the BSC," I added.

"I know," Kristy replied. "And we'll never be as famous as the We Love Kids Club."

Uh-oh. I didn't want to get into *that*.

"But that's okay," Kristy went on. "Fame isn't so important." She took a deep breath. "I was actually jealous of your group for awhile. Can you believe that?"

"Really?" (I was glad Kristy couldn't see the smile on my face.) "Well, to tell you the truth, all that publicity was one huge pain in the neck. You should be proud that the BSC is doing so well without that kind of attention."

"Thanks to your brain, Kristy," Mary Anne said.

"Yeah?" Kristy replied. "Well, I guess you have a point. I mean, we're doing all right."

More good news. Kristy and I were friends again. I don't think she had apologized to the BSC, but that was okay.

With Kristy, you take what you can get.

CHAPTER 15

"**H**ey, Dawn!" Jeff came running into my room. "What did the man say who wanted to taste some roasted goat at a restaurant?"

I looked up from my homework. "I don't know, Jeff. I've never ordered it, myself."

"It's a *joke*!" (What a surprise.) "Please pass the butt-er! *Get it?* Because a goat *butts*, and he said — "

"I get it! Now let me do my homework. Go call Robin Williams or something."

"That wasn't funny," Jeff said, stalking out.

It was six-thirty. Dad and Carol had gone out for an early dinner, and they probably wouldn't be back before eight-thirty or nine. So I was doomed to spend two more hours in a house with the worst joke-teller on the West Coast. Very soon I would actually have to endure a meal with him.

Pure torture.

Before long I couldn't stand the hunger.

I closed my books and headed for the kitchen.

That was when I heard the familiar *click* of a key in the front door, and Dad's muffled voice outside.

Salvation!

Jeff wandered into the kitchen. "What are they doing home so early?"

I heard the front door swing open. "No, of course you don't see my point," Dad was saying. "You're still wrapped up in your fantasy."

"Fantasy?" Carol sounded shocked. "Is it a *fantasy* to want to see a movie once in a blue moon? Is it a fantasy to want to spend a little time with the person you're going to marry?"

"Uh-oh," Jeff muttered.

"I think we'd better get out of the way," I said. "Follow me."

I ran into my bedroom, with Jeff at my heels. We shut the door softly behind us.

"Face reality, Carol." Dad's voice rang through the house. "I'm not a college kid. I have a family. You knew that when you met me."

"Well, what am *I*? We're getting married, Jack, so that makes me family, too! Is there, like, some rating system — kids first, divorced wife second, new wife at the bottom of the heap?"

"Carol, you couldn't be at the bottom of any

heap. You'd push yourself right to the top!"

"And what do you mean by *that*?"

Jeff and I were crouched near the door. "That sounds like a compliment to me," my brother whispered.

"It's not," I said. "Sssshh."

"Carol, we go out once or twice a week. And you're over at the house just about every day. Soon you'll be living here. What more do you want? Restaurant-hopping every night? We're both a little too old for that."

"Speak for yourself."

"*That* wasn't a compliment," Jeff informed me.

SLAM! went the door to Dad's bedroom. The argument became muffled, but if they thought they were out of earshot, they were wrong.

I heard Dad call Carol immature. I heard her call him preoccupied. Soon they were practically screaming.

Then suddenly they stopped. Jeff's eyes widened. "Did they kill each other?"

"Sssshh."

Carol was sobbing. Dad's voice grew soft and comforting. I breathed a sigh of relief.

"Oooh, they're *making up*," Jeff said with a wicked grin.

I finally opened my bedroom door. We

stepped out of our prison. (That's what it felt like.)

"Come on," I said to Jeff, "let's get something to eat."

We rummaged around in the refrigerator. I took out a yummy-looking salad. Jeff found cheese and bread and frozen fish sticks.

Just as we were sitting down, I heard Dad's bedroom door open.

A wad of chewed carrot caught in my throat. I coughed and swallowed.

Carol walked into the kitchen. Her eyes were dry, but she looked tired and glum. "Good night, Dawn. Good night, Jeff," she said.

I was glad she and Dad had made up. The argument had been scary. "See you tomorrow," I replied, trying to sound cheerful.

Carol was already halfway to the front door. "Good-bye," was all she said.

Jeff and I looked at Dad. He was leaning against the kitchen door frame, looking at the floor.

He shifted his weight and let out a sigh. Then he glanced at us. His eyes were glazed. "Kids, Carol and I have decided to stop seeing each other."

His words hung in the air for a moment.

"You mean the engagement is off?" I asked.

"No, the whole *relationship* is off."

Be careful what you wish for. It might come true. The words popped into my head, just as I'd seen them in Mal's letter. It was something Vanessa had said to Nicky.

I had gotten my wish.

I felt dizzy. None of this would have happened if I hadn't been such a spoiled baby.

"I'm so sorry, Dad," I managed to say. "I didn't want this."

Dad sat down next to me. He smiled, but his eyes were still sad. "It's not your fault, Sunshine. We just weren't meant to be married, that's all."

"Oh, Dad, I know my trip to Connecticut has something to do with it," I said. "I know what it did to Carol."

"Listen, Dawn. Carol and I had problems long ago. Your trip brought some things to a head, that's for sure. But now it's clear to me that we'd have broken up eventually anyway. You may even have done us a favor. It would have been worse to go ahead with the wedding. You know what it's like to break up *after* you're married."

"Much worse," Jeff agreed.

We ate dinner together, hardly saying a word. Part of me felt happy. Carol was out of my life, where I'd wanted her to be for a long time. But most of me felt awfully guilty. I had no business driving Dad and Carol apart. Even if it was meant to happen, it should have happened by itself.

I think Jeff knew how I was feeling. He didn't tell one joke the rest of the night. Then, before he went to bed, he came into my room and said, "Don't worry, Dawn. Maybe they'll get back together."

I smiled. "Yeah, maybe. Thanks."

He said good night and headed for his room. As I got ready for bed, I thought about the future. Maybe Dad would get back together with Carol. Maybe he'd find another girlfriend he wanted to marry. Sooner or later, the situation was bound to come up again. What would I do?

Maybe I'd be in Connecticut by then. If not, I know one thing for sure. I would deal with it. Maturely. Calmly.

But before I sank into bed, I found the piece of paper on which I'd written Dad's credit card number. I ripped it into little pieces and let them drop into the trash basket.

Just in case.

About the Author

ANN M. MARTIN did *a lot* of baby-sitting when she was growing up in Princeton, New Jersey. She is a former editor of books for children, and was graduated from Smith College.

Ms. Martin lives in New York City with her cats, Mouse and Rosie. She likes ice cream and *I Love Lucy*; and she hates to cook.

Ann Martin's Apple Paperbacks include *Yours Turly, Shirley; Ten Kids, No Pets; With You and Without You; Bummer Summer*; and all the other books in the Baby-sitters Club series.

Look for BSC #73

MARY ANNE AND MISS PRISS

We reached Burnt Hill Road again and strolled over to my old street, where we spied Jamie Newton in his front yard, doing his best to master a hula hoop that was almost as big as he was. We watched him for a few minutes as, time after time, he spun the hoop and wriggled his hips frantically, trying without success to keep the big plastic circle from dropping to the ground.

"You're spinning it too fast," Jenny called. "Go slower."

Jamie, who is a very sweet four-year-old, offered the hoop to Jenny. "Here," he said. "You show me how to do it."

"Ew! No!" Jenny leapt backwards like he had just thrust a snake in her face. "Get it away from me!"

I saw the puzzled look on Jamie's face and tried to explain, though I didn't really think he'd understand. "Jenny's worried the hoop might smudge her outfit."

"Oh." Jamie shrugged and, looping the hoop over his head, turned his back on Jenny. "Then I get the hula hoop all to myself."

I took a deep breath. "I guess we better go home."

The minute we got back inside the Prezzioso house, Jenny raced to the bathroom and washed her hands. Carefully, she squeezed the soap into her palm, and then slowly scrubbed her hands. She even checked under her fingernails. If her mother hadn't come home a few minutes later, I bet Jenny would have started another round of washing.

I said good-bye to Jenny, promising to see her tomorrow. On my way home, I realized that I'd forgotten to ask Mrs. Prezzioso why she needed a sitter every weekday. I made a mental note to ask the next time. Then I thought about Jenny's strange behavior — changing her clothes for no reason, washing and rewashing her hands. It was a bit much, even for Jenny. What had gotten into her? The only thing I knew for certain was that baby-sitting for Miss Priss on a regular basis was going to be a real challenge.

**Don't miss any of the latest books
in the Baby-sitters Club series
by Ann M. Martin**

THE BABY-SITTERS CLUB®

by Ann M. Martin

More titles... ▶

The Baby-sitters Club titles continued...

Available wherever you buy books...or use this order form.

Scholastic Inc., P.O. Box 7502, 2931 E. McCarty Street, Jefferson City, MO 65102

Please send me the books I have checked above. I am enclosing $——————
(please add $2.00 to cover shipping and handling). Send check or money order - no
cash or C.O.D.s please.

Name ——————————————————————————————————

Address ————————————————————————————————

City——————————————— State/Zip ——————————
Please allow four to six weeks for delivery. Offer good in the U.S. only. Sorry, mail orders are not
available to residents of Canada. Prices subject to change.

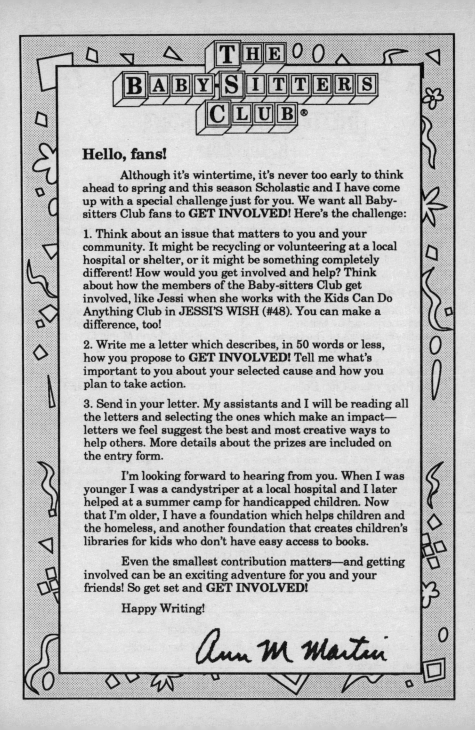

THE BABY-SITTERS CLUB®

Hello, fans!

Although it's wintertime, it's never too early to think ahead to spring and this season Scholastic and I have come up with a special challenge just for you. We want all Baby-sitters Club fans to **GET INVOLVED!** Here's the challenge:

1. Think about an issue that matters to you and your community. It might be recycling or volunteering at a local hospital or shelter, or it might be something completely different! How would you get involved and help? Think about how the members of the Baby-sitters Club get involved, like Jessi when she works with the Kids Can Do Anything Club in JESSI'S WISH (#48). You can make a difference, too!

2. Write me a letter which describes, in 50 words or less, how you propose to **GET INVOLVED!** Tell me what's important to you about your selected cause and how you plan to take action.

3. Send in your letter. My assistants and I will be reading all the letters and selecting the ones which make an impact— letters we feel suggest the best and most creative ways to help others. More details about the prizes are included on the entry form.

I'm looking forward to hearing from you. When I was younger I was a candystriper at a local hospital and I later helped at a summer camp for handicapped children. Now that I'm older, I have a foundation which helps children and the homeless, and another foundation that creates children's libraries for kids who don't have easy access to books.

Even the smallest contribution matters—and getting involved can be an exciting adventure for you and your friends! So get set and **GET INVOLVED!**

Happy Writing!

Ann M. Martin

GET INVOLVED!

IT'S THE BABY-SITTERS CLUB®

WINTER CHALLENGE!

If you're a BSC fan, you know that the Baby-sitters are always active and busy in their community...and not just with baby-sitting. When Stoney-brook needs help, the girls are ready to pitch in. If you're concerned about the town you live in, write a one-page letter about 50 words telling us your plan for improving it.

ENTER AND YOU CAN WIN:

GRAND PRIZE

- A $10,000 US Scholarship Savings Bond sponsored by Milton Bradley®, makers of The Baby-sitters Club Board Game and The Baby-sitters Club Mystery Game, and Kenner Products, makers of The Baby-sitters Club Dolls.

2 FIRST PRIZES

- A book dedicated to you, your cause and your community.
- A visit from Ann Martin to your hometown and local bookstore for an autographing and lunch.
- Plus..loads of quality BSC merchandise and a **BSC GET INVOLVED** sweatshirt, signed by Ann Martin.

100 RUNNERS-UP:
Win a **BSC GET INVOLVED** sweatshirt.

Just fill in the coupon below or write the information on a 3" x 5" piece of paper and mail with your **"GET INVOLVED"** letter to the appropriate address. U.S. Residents send entries to: **SCHOLASTIC INC., BSC WINTER CHALLENGE**, P.O. Box 742, Cooper Station, NY 10276. Canadian residents send entries to Iris Ferguson, Scholastic Inc., 123 Newkirk Road, Richmond Hill, Ontario, Canada LAC 3G5.

Rules: Entries must be postmarked by March 31, 1994. Winners will be judged by Scholastic Inc., and Ann M. Martin and notified by mail. No purchase necessary. Valid in the U.S. and Canada. Void where prohibited. Employees of Scholastic Inc., its agencies, affiliates, subsidiaries, and their immediate families are not eligible. For a complete list of winners, send a self-addressed stamped envelope after March 31, 1994. to: THE BSC WINTER CHALLENGE Winners List, at either address provided above.

- -

Attach this coupon to your **GET INVOLVED!** Letter.
THE BABY-SITTERS CLUB WINTER CHALLENGE

Name _____ Birthdate _____

Address _____ Phone# _____

City _____ State/Zip _____

Where did you buy this book? ❑ Bookstore   ❑ Other (Specify) _____

Name of Bookstore _____

HAVE YOU JOINED THE BSC FAN CLUB YET! See back of this book for details.

BSC993

Now THE BABY-SITTERS CLUB®
★ is a Video Club too! ★

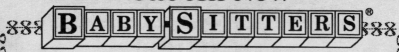

Create Your Own Mystery Stories!

MYSTERY GAME !

WHO: Boyfriend   **WHY:** Romance
WHAT: Phone Call   **WHERE:** Dance

Use the special Mystery Case card to pick WHO did it, WHAT was involved, WHY it happened and WHERE it happened. Then dial secret words on your Mystery Wheels to add to the story! Travel around the special Stoneybrook map gameboard to uncover your friends' secret word clues! Finish four baby-sitting jobs and find out all the words to win. Then have everyone join in to tell the story!

**YOU'LL FIND THIS
GREAT MILTON BRADLEY GAME
AT TOY STORES AND BOOKSTORES
NEAR YOU!**
